Road to the New Horizon

BOBBY BRAZIL

Road to the
New Horizon

All rights reserved. No part of this book may be reproduced in any form or by any electronic or mechanical means or used in any manner without written permission from the author, except for the use of short quotations in a book review.

Table of Contents

Chapter 1: Grandma, My Superhero 1

Chapter 2: Life after Grandma 13

Chapter 3: My Friend, Nobby 19

Chapter 4: Hallucinations 34

Chapter 5: Abductions 46

Chapter 6: Apparition of the Great Ali 57

Chapter 7: Cattle Pens 62

Chapter 8: Rebellion 71

Chapter 9: Planet Diaz 87

Chapter 10: My Life as a Nayzic 97

Chapter 11: Vegan Hospitality 108

Chapter 12: Rise to Fame 125

Chapter 13: The Trial 132

Chapter 14: Leaving Arielle 140

Chapter 15: The Journey Home 142

Chapter 16: Western Strands Hotel 148

Chapter 17: Home, Sweet Home 154

Chapter 18: Nobby, the Human 159

Chapter 19: Cosmological Prodigy 174

Chapter 20: Animal Lives Count 190

Chapter 21: Lake Naivasha 2040 198

Chapter 1: Grandma, My Superhero

It was the year 2040, one in which global warming and pollution were no longer an issue. At last, there was clean water for all, bountiful food for all living things and everyone had sustainable shelter from the elements. There were no wars or hunger.

As unbelievable as it would have seemed just twenty years earlier, by now, a tree or any living organism was considered more valuable than a bar of gold, any form of plant or animal more precious than the rarest gemstone.

Life itself was no longer under threat; man seemed to have made peace with all manner of other life forms and assumed the role of care takers of the planet.

Yet for me there was still sad news, regardless.

You see, Isabel, my dear wife, had passed on, along with my best friend Nobby.

I was missing them more than anything and was desperate for a diversion, for something to happen that could, even for a minuscule moment, help me to forget.

And then, just as when I'd been in my twenties, the old wanderlust struck, the urge to get out, get away, see more, do more.

But how was that even possible for an old man like me?

Then seventy-nine and just about to have my next birthday, I was too old for travelling and adventures. And I was still believing it on that day, the one on which I turned on the television to catch the tail end of an African wildlife documentary.

The sun was shining, and most of all, the sights seemed to be plentiful and fine.

Why not book a safari? I thought. *All-inclusive. They'll do everything for me; I won't have to plan any of it and won't even lift a finger, except maybe to open a few cold beers.*

***

To get the requisite 'over-sixties' experience, of course—and to avoid landing among a bunch of loved-up honeymoon couples who may well have found my presence off-putting—my booking was made via an agent specialising in trips for adventurous souls in their twilight years. And now, barely a couple of months later, there I was, the sun beating down on my poor excuse for a hat, purchased in a dusty road's tourist booth.

We started in Nairobi and before too long, we were observing lions, cheetahs, elephants, zebras, and hippos from the safety of a ramshackle four-by-four with an overhead canvas canopy.

In the Serengeti National Park, we got to watch the massive annual migration of the wildebeest and zebras, along with seeing large elephant herds lazily meandering to their nearest watering holes just as the sun dipped again on the horizon. It oddly reminded me of all the blokes back in Ireland who couldn't resist a pint in the pub on their way home from work.

This safari trip was turning out to be remarkably well organised; we rose early and slept early too, these wilderness beasts never being ones for a lie-in.

But that suited me; the huge frogs and crickets made such a racket at dawn each day that I'd be up by five anyway, waiting out front to be picked up for the day's outing.

The only thing different from what I'd been envisaging back home was the accommodation. It was not some luxury hotel after all, but in a way, this was preferable since we were spending our nights in a Kenyan safari lodge in a national park, right in the thick of things. That's exactly what we'd been doing on the final leg of our safari, now heading for our final stop, Lake Naivasha, a freshwater lake. We set out in a holiday cruiser to see the flamingos and as many hippos as we could.

It was a wonderful day but between the stifling heat and the pre-dawn start, by the time I got back to the lodge, my eighty-year-old body was exhausted.

So, it was all I could do to shower and make my way to the bar for a cold beer.

Then I joined the rest of the safari group in the restaurant for our final dinner. It was as good a meal as ever, washed down with a bottle of no doubt cheap red wine, but it tasted great under the African sun. After that, I ordered myself a brandy and, for the first time in decades, a packet of small, tipped cigars. I went outside to the deck and sat alone on soft cushions in a rocking chair, watching the bright sun fade and sink into the lake, only to be replaced by stars slowly filling the sky and the sounds of hooting owls, hyenas 'laughing', and crickets and frogs in their never-ending dusk song.

An old, thin Kenyan woman wearing an apron was sitting not far away by the kitchen door. She looked tired, as if she'd just finished a hard day's cooking. Leaning against her shoulder was a young Kenyan boy who might have been her grandson.

He looked at her and spoke; she nodded, then he got up and returned with a cup of tea on a saucer. She sipped it slowly and he snuggled back in beside her.

I lifted the small cigar to my lips, pulled on it, and blew smoke rings up to the sky. As they dissolved into the still and balmy air, memories of my own maternal grandma came to me. She had always liked to drink tea, so as soon as I'd learned how to make it, I would follow her around, asking her if she would like a cup.

Her soft, calm face would smile at me every time I asked.

She had come to live with our family soon after I was born; my mother had been admitted to hospital and had to stay there for months because of issues with her bones.

Eventually discharged, she was still far from well, spending most of the day in bed.

It had been Grandma who'd looked after all of us—my mother, my young sister, two older brothers, my father and me—throughout that period, doing all the cooking, cleaning, and housework. She seemed content to do so.

I idolised my grandma; she was always fun, fascinating me with all her stories, many of which I remembered to this day. Her earliest memory was that of her uncles in army uniform lifting her from her playpen to hug her before they went off to fight for the British empire. She said she recalled Queen Victoria coming to visit Dublin in 1900 too.

She had only been eight at the time, and with all the excitement and preparations, she had expected something magical to happen, thinking that a queen was some sort of fairy. Recalling the story of the horse-drawn coach passing by, and an old grey woman wearing black simply waving a black-gloved hand out the window, she laughed heartily, describing the innocence of her enormous disappointment.

At the age of twelve, she was sent up to Belfast to train as a nurse and went on to serve in the First World War; she worked as a casualty clearance station nurse behind the front lines, living and working in tents. When the fighting was heavy, she was up night and day. Once, when the enemy was advancing, she had to retreat by crawling through the mud like a crocodile in her nurse's pinafore dress and wearing her gas mask, listening all the time to shells whistling and exploding around.

She told me the story of her first Christmas Eve along the front when the sound of rifles firing and shells exploding stopped, replaced by German and Allied troops singing joyous Christmas carols to each other across the lines.

At the first light of dawn on Christmas Day, some German soldiers had emerged from their trenches and approached the Allied lines across no-man's land, calling out 'Merry Christmas!' Seeing the Germans unarmed, the British soldiers climbed out of their trenches to shake hands with the enemy. The generals threatened the troops with being court-martialled if they ever left their posts again.

Ah, she sighed. The poor men just wanted peace and to go home to their families.

We really looked forward to Christmas when I was growing up.

Every year, we got four live turkeys delivered off the back of a truck to our semi-detached house in a housing estate from Uncle Conan's farm. They arrived early to mid-December. We kept them in the back garden, gave them names, fed them scraps from the table if there were any, but we made sure that we found food for them so that they never went hungry.

Looking out and knocking from the kitchen window, Grandma would shout. 'Don't be getting too friendly with those birds.'

A week before Christmas, our neighbour, Mr. Murphy, a small, wiry country man who lived and worked in Dublin as a plasterer, would arrive at the house with a short piece of scaffolding pole, and a bottle of whiskey which he and my grandmother would open and have a glass or two while they joked and laughed with each other.

I'd sit quietly listening, anxious and dreading what was going to happen next.

When the glasses were emptied, we would go outside to the turkeys. I'd help Mr Murphy catch one, he would then wrap a long towel around the body of the bird to stop the wings flapping and carry it to the garden shed where Grandma was waiting with the scaffolding pole. Then, kneeling, Mr Murphy would turn the bird to face away from him, holding its head and neck to the ground.

Grandma would place the scaffolding pole directly behind the bird's head, then stand on each end of the pole in her army-issued indestructible looking thunder boots trapping the poor birds neck between the pole and the concrete floor. She was tall and heavy but still asked for me to stand beside her so she could hold onto me to keep her feet.

With a steady pull on the bird, Mr Murphy would calmly and assuredly break its neck, then hold onto it until all flapping and twitching ceased. It was a traumatic sight for me to see the birds that I was fond of being killed but one I had to grow accustomed to; these were hard times, and having a turkey was a treat. I Dublin in the 70's people generally had enough to eat, but Christmas time was when you got to eat as much as you wanted, and we all looked forward to that.

When all four turkeys were dead, Grandma would cut their throats and hang them to bleed in the garden shed, safely out of reach of pests and cats. She would have them all plucked before the neighbours came to collect their birds on Christmas Eve.

On school days, after she had checked that I had finished my homework, we would sit together on the couch as I watched my favourite TV shows. The six o'clock evening news was what she was waiting on, and I would sit quietly when it came on.

If ever I dared make a racket of some sort, or even say something to her, I would anticipate her raised hand in a 'shush' motion, shutting me up until the TV was off.

One evening, as we watched, a bishop came on to talk about an upcoming Easter event. I was watching as

Grandma's eyes narrowed to slits. Her jaw clenched and she somehow tried to speak through closed teeth. 'Would you look at that big bacon and cabbage head, the filthy hypocrite! I know what I'd do with that bastard, so I do.'

Then she looked me in the eyes. 'Remember this, Paddy, my lovely boy. Most people in this world are good, hard-working people, and they're the ones that you want to keep company with. But there are some bastards that would do you harm, and when you come across them, you must fight them, Paddy. Hit them hard and keep walloping them until they know to stay well away from you.'

I had never heard her curse before and thought it strange to see her angry.

So, I did the only thing I knew how, which was to say, 'Grandma, would you like a cup of tea?' Those words always brought a smile back to her face, and right now was no different. I carried those angry words and advice with me for the rest of my life.

My mother had made a full recovery by the time I was ten years old, and once she was back on her feet, she resumed her role as woman of the house.

That was great news, but the death of Uncle Conan from tuberculosis that year was felt throughout the household, particularly in the run-up to Christmas.

Uncle Conan's farm could no longer be the source of our seasonal bird. My father volunteered to get the turkey that year, and no one ever questioned where he might be planning to get one.

He came home from the pub the day before Christmas Eve with what he was told was a turkey from a fella he knew. I could tell it was not as good a bird as Uncle Conan's.

Traditionally, my grandmother would clean out the bird using the stock from boiling up the neck, liver and kidneys to make celery sauce. Her face when she saw this peculiar specimen was an absolute picture. She said, 'It's the strangest-looking shape, don't you think? Are you sure it's not a swan? Well, I suppose it will have to do.'

'Do? Of course, it will do. Anyway, don't be so daft,' Father said. 'Only the royals are allowed to eat swans.'

It hardly answered the question.

But as a ten-year-old boy, I believed my grandma was the wisest woman ever, and once she said it could be a swan, as far as I and the whole household were concerned, it was a swan. My brothers and I laughed, speculating as to what canal it had lived on.

Her comment had not been a joke, though we'd believed it to be at the time. No, she was deadly serious. In those days, poaching was a big thing, a lot of folk pilfering whatever they could get their hungry hands on because times were lean.

Mam was furious at the very thought that we could be eating wild swan from the canal on Christmas Day. Her patience had already grown thin because of all the time and money my father had been spending in the pub. 'Honest to God, can't you just buy one from the butcher like everybody else? Then, at least we know what we're eating!'

The bird had not been plucked well either, so Grandma got out what she called her 'tool kit', a pair of hefty pliers and a screwdriver to remove the remaining feathers.

I could still picture her sitting at the kitchen table, staring through thick-rimmed glasses, wearing her home-knitted cardigan, apron and tartan skirt, patiently plucking away with pliers. I wasn't sure why the screwdriver came in handy, but she was so very proud of it, having acquired it by confronting a burglar trying to break into the house in the middle of the night. She showed off that tool at every opportunity.

We loved to hear the story of how, sleeping on the sofa downstairs, she'd heard the burglar at the window, scratching and tapping to see where he could get in best.

She took everything in her stride, Grandma did, so I could just picture her heaving an exasperated sigh as that wretched crook disturbed her slumber.

Rather than wake the four men upstairs, she just dealt with the nuisance herself.

She boasted that she had sent him running, and he'd dropped the screwdriver because of the awful fright when she roared at him. She found that tool underneath the windowsill the very next morning, reposing in the dirt where it had landed.

My mother stewed over the thought of eating swan for the days leading up to Christmas, a palpable anger building up in her. So, it would be more than fair to say Christmas dinner was a tense affair, all sitting eagerly watching as she carved the bird.

There was such a tension in the air, all waiting for the inevitable backlash.

My father sat looking like he was in court, waiting to be sentenced.

His defence, apparently based on the grounds that he'd been told it was just a different breed of turkey, was clearly not working.

My brother Cian was the first to be served. 'This turkey's a bit tough,' he joked, knowing full well the effect that this statement would have. He tried to hold in a laugh.

With that, my mother exploded with anger, hurling his plate of 'a different breed of turkey' into the open fire where it went up with a big plume of angry smoke, hissing and popping as it did. She then reached for the remaining dinners on the table, her lean fingers grasping and grabbing as we each slid our plates out of the way, hanging on tightly to ours. We didn't care; turkey or swan, we were eating it.

Grandma turned to my mother and ordered, 'Will ye just calm down? It's done now. Whatever the bird is, it's dead, and it won't be coming back, so just let them eat it.'

When she spoke, people listened although she must have had her hands full with our fiery mother. Her fierce temper was known to everyone. She never even bothered denying her short fuse, simply replying, 'So long as you know.'

I took this to mean, 'You had better watch out around me, boy.'

My tall skinny father in contrast, a pacifist by nature, he always said I had inherited my mother's temper and her stubbornness too. One day, he said, it would get me into trouble. He wouldn't have known at that time how right he would be.

In the O'Reilly household, my mother was the sergeant major, issuing instructions that had to be instantly obeyed. In her mind, everything she said and did was right, and anything my father said or did was wrong.

She also did all the jobs, carpentry, painting, and decorating.

My father joked, 'If I so much as stand near a wall where she's painting, I'll be painted over.' So, he kept out of the way, calmly retiring to the pub to his friends at the end of each day. After a restorative dose of Guinness, he would then drive home and head straight for his armchair again, where my mother would bring him his dinner on a tray while he watched whatever sport was on. When he had nearly finished eating, she would appear in a flash, whip the tray from him and wash up his dishes.

My sister Mary, seven years younger than me, would sit on his lap and tell him how her day had gone. One day, as soon as he stepped foot through the door, she complained, 'Mammy hit me on the head with the pan.'

In those days, most children got slapped by their parents for misbehaving, but my father never raised a hand to us. He left the disciplining of the family to my mother, and I never got away with anything lightly. He was furious, however, when he heard what had happened to his precious Mary. He marched straight to the kitchen.

'You have gone too far this time!' he shouted. 'You need to curb that temper of yours or you'll end up in jail!'

'What did Mary tell you now?' she asked, smiling back at him.

'She said that you hit her with the pan.'

'Yes, I did! I tapped her on the head with the soft fresh white pan of bread. You didn't think I hit her on the head with the frying pan now, did you?'

My mother started to giggle and before long, they were both laughing hysterically.

That's the way it was in our house; my mother and father fighting one minute, and the next, it was all laughter and smiles.

People often commented on how much my parents fought and were at odds but also on how much they loved each other despite such polarised temperaments.

Grandma did not interfere in their daily disputes, but her presence in the house ensured their rows didn't escalate too far.

My father was very fond of his mother-in-law, bringing her home baby bottles of whiskey from the pub. They shared a great love for sport; her favourites were horse racing, boxing and rugby, and on the weekend, Dad would place the bets for her.

As I got older, I stopped following Grandma around and asking if she wanted cups of tea, but every day, I would enquire what she was up to as she always had some sort of project on the go. She loved gardening. Our house backed onto a railway line, and Grandma was constantly at war with the weeds and brambles springing up wildly from it, encroaching upon our garden.

I also helped her battle with all the thorns and barbed wire. One day, as we worked, she noticed a silver birch tree sapling, all choked and twisted from the scutch around, on the railway line side of the barbed wire fence. We set out to rescue it. I cleared the jungle around the sapling, and she straightened and staked it.

With beads of sweat running down her forehead, she said, 'That will grow to be a fine tree. But I'd better go in now …'

Halfway down the garden path, she fell, perhaps dizzy from the effort of all that gardening. I ran to her, turning her on her back.

'Grandma, Grandma, wake up!'

But she never did.

A spring breeze rained blossoms onto us from the cherry tree as she released her final breath.

That silver birch sapling did grow to be the finest tree, just as she'd predicted. The neighbours once asked if we could cut it down as it was blocking the sunlight in their garden. I explained why I simply couldn't, and they never asked again.

Chapter 2: Life after Grandma

After Grandma died, there was no calming influence in the house, the fights between my mother and father intensifying.

My mother believed that my father had been spoilt as a child, which was the reason he always put himself first. She had married a man with a good job and a promising career, so she dreamed of living in a large house with all the trappings of wealth.

Things had not gone in that direction, of course. Far from it.

All the money he earned was being spent on Guinness, sports and gambling.

He worked in advertising, often leading to late nights at corporate promotion events.

Then there was his interest in football.

As a founder member of our local Gaelic football club, he'd participate in just about everything going on there and everywhere else. 'If people participated in their community, the world would be a happier place,' he'd say.

My mother did not share his view. 'Pity you don't participate in your own house,' she would reply. She felt she was left with all the household responsibilities without anywhere near enough money to run it. So, when eventually he did come home at night, there would be a fight, if not immediately in front of the children, then later.

It often ensued just as we were trying to fall asleep.

The fights became fiercer and more bitter. I loved them both, however, always desperately thinking of ways to make them happy. Instead of listening and paying attention in the classroom, my thoughts invariably fixated on my unhappy home.

One night, lying awake with all the shouting going on downstairs, I decided to confront them with an idea I had long been nurturing.

Down the stairs I went in my pyjamas to the sitting room.

My mother was jabbing an accusing finger at my father as he sat in his armchair.

I looked from one to the other. 'I know you drink lots of Guinness,' I told Dad. 'If you drank a few pints less every day and smoked only half as many cigarettes, you could give the money saved to Mam. Then, the money problem's solved.'

I truly hoped they would say 'Thank you, Paddy, for your clever suggestion. It was helpful,' but instead, they both just laughed in my face.

I went back up to bed, deeply wounded.

Soon after that night, they had a fight in front of all of us which ended with them threatening to split and take two children each.

Looking back, it was just something said in the heat of their argument, but the threat of the family breaking up upset me to my core.

From being an agreeable boy and the best student in the class, I turned into a surliest with the lowest marks, rebelling against everything. When the school reports came home, my parents couldn't understand what had happened. I had changed and was now troubled, keeping company with others who were trouble like me.

Bullying was commonplace in school back then, fights breaking out first thing in the morning as we waited for the school bell. We would line up in two rows on the bench along the length of the bicycle shed. The two boys at the front of each row fought to see who could throw off the other whilst still managing to stay on the bench himself.

If your opponent held onto you and you fell off the bench with him, you continued the fight on the ground. When the fight was over, you had to rejoin the queue at the back end of the bench and move forward to fight again.

We loved fighting and watching boxing matches on our black and white TVs.

Families would get up in the middle of the night to watch the live streaming of the fights in the classic heavyweight boxing championship.

Muhammad Ali, Smokin' Joe Frazier and George Foreman were kings, and we re-enacted their fights in the school yard the following mornings.

There were fifty-four boys in each class, the teachers keeping order by fear.

One had a clock and he frequently put it to use, threatening us.

'If I can't hear that clock ticking, you will all be sorry.'

If there was any noise in his class, he would grab hold of and beat a few random boys until he felt sure he had knocked the high spirits out of us all and the room was again quiet enough for him to teach. I never bore any grudge against those teachers.

Whether lay teachers or priests, it made no difference; that was simply the way to control an unruly class in those days. We knew well not to go home and tell our parents we had been beaten, lest they accuse us of deserving it and give us another one.

And in those days, if you were crying, that was when your mother or father would say, 'Shut up or I'll give you something to cry about'.

At school break times, arguments would often erupt over who was the best fighter in the school. My name often came up simply due to ranking among the bigger boys and the hardest to throw off the bench at the bicycle shed. Without consulting me or my proposed opponent, fights were often arranged by the smaller boys for after school.

In the beginning, I dreaded them. All I wanted was to go home and do my homework. But soon, with my reputation soaring and my popularity on the rise, I began to enjoy the roars of the boys and the admiration of all my pals afterwards.

Our fights took place on a patch of grass in the church grounds, a convenient little spot that we called *Madison Square Garden,* after the New York location for the real heavyweight title fights. There, the only kid I could not easily beat was a coffee-coloured boy, Gyt Camero, nicknamed 'Choc Ice'. His father was an African American US Army GI, who got together with his mother, an Irish factory worker, in London during the Second World War. For just fourteen, Gyt was stocky.

I was still only twelve.

Gyt's parents decided that he should do two extra years in primary school, after which point he would be legally old enough to leave school and work with his father on his bread van, delivering fresh-baked loaves and buns door to door.

In my mind, it was Gyt as Joe Frazier versus me, Muhammad Ali. When we fought, I danced and punched, goading him at the same time. Imitating Ali, I had the nerve to call him ugly, and the hundred or so boys pushing and pulling for a ringside view would laugh at the taunts and yell, encouraging us to 'beat the hell out of each other'.

Either of us could have ended the fight by simply saying, 'I give in'.

But to say those words was to accept defeat, and neither of us would ever contemplate throwing in the towel. The fight could only be stopped by the priests, schoolteachers, or the police from the nearby police station. We had many fights during our last year in primary school, and the finale, billed as *The Hammer O'Reilly versus The Choc Ice Camero*, surpassed all the spectators' expectations.

As usual, we began by exchanging punches, then we clinched and began to bear-wrestle. I wrapped my right arm around his neck, locking his head against the side of my body. I held his head tight until my arm began to tire and he broke free.

As he did so, he bent down, picked up a heavy rotting tree branch, breaking it across my back. The blow buckled and winded me, I fell down on one knee to regain my breath before resuming the contest. There were boos and jeering from the crowd; you didn't use sticks, we had rules, and he had broken them.

Grandma was long dead, but in that moment, I saw her with the same angry face she had worn when we'd watched the bishop on the news.

The words she had spoken at the time came flooding back.

'Remember this, Paddy, my lovely boy, most people are good in this world but …'

This is what she must have meant. He wasn't getting away with it. As I began to rise from my knees, I swung my right shoulder back.

'You're one ugly bastard!' I shouted, and with all the vengeance in my bones, I spun forward. The joint forces of that spin, combined with the strength of my rising legs, went through my knuckles to land a perfectly aimed trademark hammer punch right on his nose, I felt it and heard it break as he then fell to his knees.

He was clutching onto his nose as if it would disintegrate if he took his hand away, and I'd never forget the sight of all that blood streaming through his fingers, nor the sound of him, spitting and coughing as the blood spatters flew everywhere. The fight was over.

'Go on, you good thing. You'll never beat The Hammer O'Reilly!' my supporters chanted as they ran to clap me on the back.

I didn't intend to do him such harm, I didn't sleep well that night. I had nothing against Choc ice, he probably just wanted to go peacefully home but that's not the way things went in School O'Connells.

That was my last fight in primary school. After that, I would soon be heading to a more affluent boys' school for my secondary education, though why they accepted me with such a reputation, I would never know. Perhaps they had never checked up.

In the final year of school, at the age of seventeen, it was time to sit my government exams, which I never much cared about at the time. Nor did I care when, on the day the results were being released, I went fishing with my friend, Nobby.

Due to not telling my mother where I was going, I would later learn she had been anxiously waiting at home to find out how I had done. Surprisingly, I did narrowly pass, enough to get myself into a government draftsman course, and when I finished that, I went on to get a job drawing reinforcement bars in concrete.

Just as it sounds, it wasn't much fun.

Chapter 3: My Friend, Nobby

I first met Nobby in the dressing room of Maywood Rugby Club. We had joined on the same day to play under-14s rugby, neither of us having played before. We gravitated towards one another immediately, perhaps because neither of us knew anyone else.

Or possibly, it was down to the fact that we were at either end of the height scales. I was tall and lean, and he was short and stocky.

Before long, I considered him to be my best friend.

He had a mixed-up accent, sometimes speaking with a distinguished tone, pronouncing each word precisely. Yet if he got excited, mostly on the rugby pitch, a strong 'Towers' accent came through. He would switch between the two, depending on where he was or in what situation he found himself.

A few weeks after we'd met, he invited me for dinner at his apartment at the Towers. I stared into his face not knowing what to say.

Because of its reputation, I didn't want to go to the Towers; everyone knew the Dobermans and Rottweilers hung around in pairs for safety there.

He looked at the ground and asked again. 'My mother asked me to invite you, so will you come?'

'Great,' I replied. 'When?'

'Next Saturday, after our match.'

When I told my mother about the invitation and that Nobby's mother was a single mother living in the Towers, she was not happy.

'Who is this Nobby?'

Like most people, she was suspicious of the Towers, knowing it was a socially deprived area with a high crime rate and a substance abuse problem. She didn't want me hanging around there. She turned to my father.

'Tommy, tell him he can't go.'

'Mary,' he said, 'I've met Nobby. He's on Paddy's rugby team, and he seems like a nice fellow to me. We have no right to stop him going, and besides, it's *how* you live, not *where* you live, that's of importance. I'll drive him up and collect him afterwards.'

***

One October afternoon, we pulled up in my father's car outside Nobby's tower block, one of eight arranged in an octagon shape. Four roads converged to meet a ring road in front of them, and inside the ring were the playing fields.

There was also a playground, some football pitches and stretches of wasteland dotted with overturned cars and kids galloping piebald ponies.

A menacing-looking pack of skinheads surveyed our car from a wall where they sat drinking cans of beer.

I looked at my father's worried face and thought that maybe he was regretting his support of the plan.

As we sat in the front seats of the car, he looked sternly at me. 'I'll see you right here at 7 p.m. sharp, OK?'

I agreed and got out, looking over my shoulder at the car as it drove away. I walked towards the tower with a sense of dread. Then I saw Nobby coming out to meet me.

'Hey, Lanky! That's a nice car your Da has,' one of the skinheads shouted.

I kept my eyes looking straight at Nobby, hoping the loser would leave me alone. But he pushed himself off the wall and sauntered forward to confront me, six pals following him. 'D'ya think he'd let us drive it?' he asked.

'No, he won't even let *me* drive it.'

'What a la-di-da accent!' he joked to his friends. 'Where you from, boy?' he asked.

'Seafield,'

'Ah, that's a lovely area. Oh, I do like to be beside the seaside,' he joked, and the gang tittered. 'Trouble is, the boys in blue won't let the likes of us go there; if dey see us, dey move us on. So, what you doin' in our shitty kip of a neighbourhood?'

In his Towers accent, Nobby told him to feck off and leave me alone.

'Ha! Look a' the two o' dem! It's the Little and Lanky Show—you boys should be in the circus!' he said. His loyal followers continued to enjoy the spectacle.

Nobby never hung around with these boys, but he knew who they were and that they meant trouble.

One grabbed Nobby, holding him in a headlock while another grabbed me by the hair. I reached and grabbed *his* hair, so we ended up with a fistful each.

He was trying to pull me to the ground to boot me in the head.

We pulled each other around and exchanged uppercuts until eventually, we just held each other's heads steady.

'Curley, hit 'im on the head wid your chain,' one of the boys called out.

I noticed a chain dangling to the ground beside Curley's boots.

Splayed into two at one end, it looked as if originally, it must have belonged to the seat of a playground swing.

I yanked the ginger head up to protect my own, his breath against my ear, hearing him gasping. This made the point to me that I was fit, and he wasn't. So, I had him, but how long could I protect myself before receiving a blow from Curley's chain?

Just then, a shout came from one of the balconies. 'Curley, your chips are ready!'

Back in the eighties, there were few shortcuts. To make chips, your mother had to peel the potatoes, cut the chips and deep fry them in a huge pan of animal fat.

It was a big deal if someone's mother was making chips, and Curley must have wanted his fresh from the pot.

'I'm off,' I heard him say. 'There's enough of youse to sort dem two out.'

'You let go of my hair, and I'll let go of yours, and we'll call it quits,' I said, naively offering ginger head a way out. Slowly and simultaneously, we relaxed our respective grips on clumps of the other's hair, standing up straight and staring at each other.

Nobby grabbed me by the arm, and we walked on. 'Don't tell me ma that this happened, will you? She's worked very hard to make this nice for you.'

'Don't worry, I won't.'

Nobby had once confided in me that he'd never met his dad. His mother had told him that his father was a German submariner with whom she'd had a short romance. Once her well-off family heard the news that their young daughter was pregnant, with the submariner nowhere to be seen, she was made to leave her family home.

She now worked as a waitress below the high-rise towers, in the Towers bar.

She was determined they would not live there for long. She paid for Nobby's elocution lessons and taught him how to play the piano, which, along with joining the rugby club, would be part of a snakes and ladders game for her to make her way back to where she had come from, a large detached Georgian house in a much sought-after area of south Dublin. My invitation to dinner, I realised later, was a step along the way.

The apartment was on the seventh of eight floors. The lift was broken, so we climbed up the stairwell through trash and the stink of urine, past walls daubed with obscene graffiti, finally walking along the corridor to his front door.

Nobby put the key in the lock and pushed the door open.

We crossed the threshold into a well-decorated, clean, sweet-smelling hall. You would never have guessed we were in the same building as the one we had just walked through. Nobby's mother must have been very houseproud. I expected it to be a 'take your shoes off' kind of home but for now, I kept them on.

Nobby's mother came to greet me.

I estimated her to be only in her mid-thirties. She was good-looking and elegant, also tall but regardless, she still had to stretch on her tippytoes to kiss me on each cheek. She held my hand warmly, then took my coat.

She hung it on a coat stand.

'Take off your shoes, too. You'll be more comfortable,' she said. Well, what a surprise. Of course, I did so, my feet suddenly in heaven as they sank into the pile of the carpet. 'Thanks for inviting me,' I said. 'Something smells lovely!'

We proceeded to the living-dining room, past an oak dining table and piano.

When Mrs Soft—we all called each other's parents by their surnames back in those days—went back into the kitchen, I moved a cushion, sat down on the couch and admired a realistic imitation log fire with its oriental hearth rug.

A living room to which just about everyone would aspire. As if the sun also knew which home to head to, bright daylight shone in on the walls through spotlessly clean windows, bathing many tropical plants which, in turn, added a sense of fresh air to the room. It was a world apart from what lay outside that front door.

I momentarily had to wonder whether I might be having an out-of-body experience, it was that surreal. But the voice of Mrs Soft pulled me back to reality.

'You must be hungry after your match. We have a crab salad as a starter and lamb as a main course. I hope you like crab and lamb?' she asked.

'I like everything, Mrs Soft. The only things I can't eat are green peppers. They don't agree with me.'

'It's good that I haven't cooked any, so.'

She shouted questions from the kitchen, asking about my likes and dislikes. I did my best to engage in conversation with her. When she eventually emerged again to talk, she squinted as she scanned my face. 'What sort of a match were you playing? You look like you've been boxing. There are bruises all over you.'

'No, no, Mrs Soft. Not boxing. We were playing rednecks from the country. They're always very rough and I did have a punch-up with one of them, that's all.'

'And what about you, Norbert? How come your face is all puffed up, too?'

'I jumped in to try and stop the fight, and I got punched too. That's all, Mam.'

Mrs Soft shook her head and then announced that dinner was ready.

Nobby pulled back the carving chair at the head of the table to show me my seat.

Beside each place setting sat a brilliant white linen napkin, folded to represent a swan—and I was thankful we were not about to eat one.

The salad fork lay outside the dinner fork on the left side of the napkin. To the right were the knives, their blades facing inwards. Everything was pristine and meticulously arranged as if Mrs Soft had passed through a swanky finishing school.

The crab salad starter was mouth-watering, and the lamb main course was equally as good. A homemade rhubarb crumble and ice cream followed for dessert.

After Nobby had cleared the table, Mrs Soft suggested he should play the piano.

'No, Mam. Paddy didn't come here to listen to me play the piano.'

'Paddy, what's your favourite song?' Mrs Soft asked, ignoring her son. All her focus seemed to be on me, and it was now clear why Nobby said his mam had gone to a lot of trouble to prepare this meal in honour of my dinner visit.

I told her I didn't have any favourite song, because I'd never considered it.

'Well then, what's your favourite film?' she asked. "You must have one of those."

'The Jungle Book?'

'Aaaah, that's a great film! When Norbert was a toddler, he would sit on my lap, and we watched that many times together. Norbert,' she pleaded. 'Play I'm the King of the Swingers.'

Nobby shot me an apologetic look.

'Go on, I like that song!' I said, trying to encourage him. It would be nice to hear and see him play. So, he started playing and we all sang along.

'Now I'm the king of the swingers,
Oh, the jungle VIP,'

When we got to the '*Oh, oobee doo*' part, Mrs Soft danced like the orangutan, and I pretended to be the bear.

'*I wanna be like you*
I wanna walk like you ...'

Nobby played, and his mother and I danced. Then, I was the elephant, using my arm as a pretend trunk, which was also a trumpet.

We did the second verse and finished with the chorus. It was amazing fun.

*'Can learn to be
Like someone like you
Can learn to be
Like someone like me!'*

Then I looked at my watch: 7:15 p.m. Dad would be waiting in the car outside.

'Mrs Soft, thank you for dinner, but I must go now. I wasn't watching the time, and I'm late...! My father will be waiting.'

'Oh dear,' she said. 'Well then, you must go. It's been marvellous to see you.'

Nobby ran down with me to see me off.

When I reached the car, a scantily clad woman was leaning over, knocking at the car window and waving in at my dad. I could see him frantically shooing her away, his face tight with fury. 'I thought I told you to be here at 7 p.m. sharp! You're late! I'm not collecting you here again if you can't be on time.'

After having such a great time, I continued to go to Nobby's apartment, at first only before lunch because the hooligan element wouldn't be getting out of bed until well into the afternoon. Our paths did cross some afternoons, but they ignored us, having learned from experience that we fought back.

***

Nobby and I played rugby together all through our school years, and when we finished school, work was hard to come by. A woman we knew from the rugby club gave both Nobby and me jobs painting and decorating her holiday home in north County Dublin. She was sure we would make the perfect double act as painters and decorators because, with me being a tall bean pole and Nobby's five-feet nothing, we were the perfect height to do both the high and low bits!

Every night, we went down to the pubs there. People noticed us because of our height difference, and after a couple of drinks, the happy holidaymakers would want to chat with us. We introduced ourselves as painting and decorating specialists, saying. I was the ceiling fella and Nobby was the skirting board dude. We amused the whole pub, drank profuse amounts of beer and picked up new clients as the bars were closing.

From the bar, we would head to holiday homes to start work. This was the way we rolled. I'd hold the paste-coated wallpaper to the top of the wall, then call to Nobby, 'Are we all right on the bottom?'

Then Nobby would call, 'Are we right at the top?'

When we both said, 'Right,' we would call, 'Stick it on.'

The results often looked OK at night through our beer goggles but not so good the following day in the stark white daylight. Then, we'd stand back, hands on hips, staring before eventually saying, 'Ah'. Somehow, not too keen on redoing it, we would manage to convince ourselves that the work would pass. Besides, holiday homes were not meant to be decorated to the same standard as 'real' homes, were they?

And so far, nobody had complained or shied away from paying us for our efforts.

We worked on the holiday homes for six weeks during the summer.

Nobby's mum was anxious while he was away and relieved and pleasantly surprised when her son came back unharmed.

The first Friday we were back, I called by Nobby's apartment, as planned, to head into Dublin city for the night to spend our hard-earned money.

I got the usual lecture from Mrs Soft.

'I never worry about my Norbert unless he is going out with you. The two of you are a double act that seems to attract trouble.'

'Don't worry, Mrs Soft! We'll be extra careful. Nothing is going to happen.'

I tried to reassure her, saying we'd been in Skerries for six weeks and not got ourselves mixed up in a single fight. I felt my cheeks take the form of a grin.

'And you're proud of that record, too!' she replied, shaking her head. She then asked Nobby if he'd put on that nice aftershave she had bought him for Christmas.

Her eyes twinkled. 'There's nothing you can do about the way you look, but at least you can smell nice.' Then she laughed.

We drank pints in a few different bars in the city before making our way to a nightclub. We had a particular routine when we tried to chat up the ladies. Since they had to look up when they were talking to me and down when talking to Nobby, we would purposely take turns asking them questions to make their heads go up and down.

After a while, they would catch on to what we were doing and laugh at our antics. So, that night as usual, we practiced our routine on two girls, all having a good time.

Not wanting the night to finish, we invited them to a late-night club, and they agreed to come. It was only close by, so I suggested, 'Hey, why don't we just walk?'

'Not in these heels!' the girls protested.

'Jump up on my back,' I told the one I fancied, 'and I'll give you a jockey back.'

Well, Nobby's girl also thought that was a good idea, jumping up on his back without warning. She was a big girl to say the least and he hadn't anticipated it.

Nobby buckled, landing head-first against a stub wall of the National Art Gallery, his face gushing blood. We had to call an ambulance—it was really that bad—and I went to the hospital with him, finding out he needed stitches in the cut over his eye and observation for concussion. The doctor took out a pen, moving it right and left, requesting Nobby to follow it with his eyes.

He had to keep his head steady at the same time. He failed the test, but the doctor concluded the cause was likely the quantity of Guinness he'd consumed. Due to that, he discharged him anyway, leaving me wondering what the point of the test was!

We got a taxi and I decided to go home with him, just in case. We arrived on a late summer's night at the Towers. On the horizon, you could make out the glimmer of the dawn of a new summer's day. We climbed the stairwell and along the corridor to his apartment door, stepping over scattered bodies that were languishing, sleeping one off.

'You know what, Paddy?' Nobby said, 'I'm starving, and my ma has eight sausages in the fridge—four each!'

I grinned. 'Better not eat them, or your ma will be making sausages out of us when she finds out we ate her breakfast!'

But he was not up for being dissuaded. His adventure had made him ravenous. There was one good thing about it, though, which was to determine he couldn't have a concussion; eating a greasy fry-up would've been the last thing on his mind if so.

His plan was to open the door quietly, sneak along the hall past his mother's bedroom and into the kitchen, then close the door of the kitchen, fry the sausages and make sandwiches. He'd get up early and go to the butcher, managing to replace them before she was any the wiser. What could possibly go wrong?

We should have gone straight to bed, but I hadn't eaten since my dinner at six o'clock the previous day either, so like a true follower, I went along with the idea. We carved a large loaf of bread into thick slices, covered them in butter, made a cup of tea and cooked the sausages. We sat there at the two-person table in Nobby's small kitchen, munching in blissful silence. Neither of us heard the door open.

Mrs Soft's voice made us jump. 'What are you two doing up at this hour? And who said you could eat those sausages? They're for tomorrow!'

Nobby was sitting with his back to the door. 'Sorry, Ma.' He looked at her over his shoulder. 'I was already planning to buy more in the morning.'

'Jesus Christ!' she said, catching sight of his face. 'What in the hell has happened to your eye?' She stepped towards him in her white dressing gown and sheepskin slippers and lifted his chin. Her face contorted in horror at the cut that ran so close to his eye.

'Don't tell me the two of you were fighting again!'

She glared at me accusingly.

'No Mam,' Nobby told her. 'A girl jumped on my back, and I fell.'

She directed another dark scowl at me.

'It wasn't my fault, Mrs Soft,' I told her. 'How can I be blamed for that?'

'Oh, it's never your fault, is it, Paddy?' She sank onto a chair and dropped her head in her hands. 'Just go home, will you! Honestly, I'm already sick of seeing your face.'

I walked home in the dawn light, feeling like it was my fault.

And she was right. Yes, it was true, something always seemed to happen when Nobby and I were out. I felt bad about eating her sausages too. But they did taste good.

***

The Towers' skinheads may have chosen to ignore us but everywhere else we went, people would habitually make fun of our heights. We felt like it was discrimination. After all, you couldn't make comments about people over the colour of their skin, or their religion, or their age, or their weight, so who decided it was OK to comment and make fun of our heights?

I had kept growing and at the age of nineteen, was 6'8" and very skinny. 6'8" may not seem that tall nowadays, but back in the eighties, people were shorter, so it would have been the equivalent of nearer 6-10" back then. From first thing in the morning until I went to sleep at night, it was a constant topic of conversation and ridicule.

Even walking down the street, people would stare and make fun of me.

Gradually, my shoulders slumped, and I began to stoop, constantly feeling so ashamed and self-conscious about my freakish, ridiculous, ungainly height.

My mam would thump me on the back in temper. 'Stand up straight! Don't slouch!'

Mrs Soft was a religious woman and one day after she had made us our lunch, she sat us down on the couch and explained something to us both.

'You, Norbert, are one of the shortest men I have ever seen, and you, Paddy, are the tallest. No two people in the world are the same; we are all an essential part of God's creation, no man better than any other. The Lord works in mysterious ways, and he obviously has a great sense of humour too, introducing you two to each other and then encouraging the pair of you to be best friends! I can hear him laughing!

'But Paddy, let me tell you something. You don't look proud of yourself when you are stooped. You should be; you're a lot to be proud about. So please stand straight.'

From that day onwards, I always walked tall and pulled my shoulders back.

We understood that we were a curiosity, and we accepted that people would comment on us, but if Nobby or I thought they were being disrespectful, we would take them on. As a result, we were always getting into fights.

We fought on street corners, at dances, outside churches. We fought just about everywhere you could think of, unwilling to be the butt of some ignorant asshole's joke for even a moment.

Through clenched teeth, I would utter these ever-reliable words, 'You're one ugly bastard!' and then aim right for the nose.

If the punch landed right, the asshole's eyes would at least water, rendering them temporarily blurry, but if the punch landed *squarely* on target with force, you could feel the nose break—tears and blood would follow, and the fight would be all over.

Mrs Soft just couldn't understand it. 'I never worry about my Norbert unless he's out with you! He always comes home roughed up,' she would say to me.

As the years passed, the fights continued, but instead of street corners, we had moved on to bars and nightclubs. On one occasion, I was queuing to get a drink at the bar when somebody made a degrading comment about my height.

'Look at the circus freak,' the wise guy said, knowing he was out of my earshot.

Nobby, following behind, heard the remark. He reached up and grabbed him by the collar and told him to shut his mouth. There was shock on the man's face.

The asshole then grabbed Nobby by his collar.

'Fucking circus dwarf, why don't you worry about yourself instead? You can earn a lot of money for being a retard in a show.'

That was enough insult for my ears. I then punched the asshole, setting a row off between me and Nobby, and the mouth and his friends.

Before long, we found ourselves getting barred from most of the local venues, soon becoming known to the police too. After being questioned and released without charge for my part in a pub brawl, I decided I had escaped charges too often; enough was enough. It was time for me to leave Dublin.

I could tell Mrs Soft was pleased to hear I was leaving for London.

The idea that her son may have ended up getting arrested along with me did not sit well with her. Her contentment, however, lasted only a couple of weeks until Nobby decided to follow me over to England.

Chapter 4: Hallucinations

We lived and played rugby together in London for three years, after which we returned home and worked in Dublin for a year. During this time, a severe bout of wanderlust struck us both, resulting in our joint decision to head for Australia.

Some friends had come home after a year of working there, captivating us with such great stories that we simply had to go.

When we landed in Perth airport, we were both twenty-nine. Of course, right away, we joined a rugby club where we were received with the warmest of Australian welcomes. This was partly due to the inclusive, all-one-family nature of the sport of rugby, and partly down to coming from Ireland

Our new friends even found us work as painters and decorators.

When the rugby season finished about two months later, we rode on the Indian Pacific train line across the Nullarbor desert to Adelaide, where we worked another month, picking grapes and drinking gargantuan quantities of wine.

From there, we visited the Blue Mountains, taking in the waterfalls, cliffs and eucalyptus forests, before travelling on to Sydney and working as concrete shuttering carpenters. We knew nothing about the job when we started, but there was a shortage of labour, and we were enthusiastic workers who managed to stay employed.

The idea behind our trip had been to see as much of the country as we could in the year, so after three months of carpentry and with pockets full of money, we travelled up the east coast, spending all our earnings in as many bars, casinos and concerts as we could manage. We sailed yachts, white-water rafted, tracked through rainforests and crossed into the forbidden lands of the indigenous people.

Finally, we caught a Greyhound bus to Mataranka Springs in the Northern Territories, famous for its warm geothermal pools. We baked on that twelve-hour trip with no air conditioning. Six months of partying since our arrival had taken their toll, and by now, our batteries were running low. All we wanted to do was eat a steak and sleep. We were longing to breathe some fresh air, but when we arrived at sundown, hot and sticky, we found ourselves in a humid jungle, the air like treacle.

'I'm knackered,' Nobby said.

I said nothing, just staring at him and managing the slightest of nods because I was knackered too, barely enough residual energy to bother replying.

'Let's just grab a beer and a bite to eat and have an early night,' I suggested.

An excited atmosphere buzzed through the campsite. People from Darwin and the local sheep stations rubbed shoulders with tourists from all over the world. The entertainment was to be provided by Wally and Friends, a local band that played popular local tunes. I had met Wally earlier at the bar; he'd gawped at my height, and we'd chatted for a moment before I rejoined Nobby at a wooden table.

Then, Wally appeared on stage, introduced his band and roared to the crowd, 'Is there anybody here from England?'

Some people politely put up their hands.

'Anybody from Scotland?'

A few more.

'Wales?'

A few more.

'USA?'

… And so on, around the world.

When Wally reached Ireland, Nobby and I yahooed, punching the air and jumping up and down, out of control for a minute or two.

We thought we might have overcooked it because some Australians started to shout, 'Go home, you Irish bastards!'

It wasn't quite the welcome we'd hoped for or received at the start of the trip.

When Nobby suggested we finish our beers and clear off to bed, I agreed.

Then Wally started to play an Aussie tune in which the audience had to participate and pretend to be kangaroos.

He shouted to a big, strapping Aussie girl who looked as though she had just finished a day of shearing sheep and hadn't had the opportunity to shower since.

'Get that big Irish fellow up to dance!' he told her.

I quickly turned my back, hoping she would take the hint, but when I looked over my shoulder, there she was, stomping towards me.

I pretended to be deep in conversation with Nobby, but she grabbed me by the scruff of the neck, pulling me up.

She had long fair hair and was wearing shorts, a black Iron Maiden singlet and flip-flops on her feet. She was very heavy, but curiously, also attractive and deeply scary at the same time. I supposed most blokes were intrigued by women who seemed in some way powerful or intimidating.

This girl was an embodiment of contradictions that worked rather well together.

'Dance with me!'

I took it as an order, not a request, thinking, *I'm going to have to go along with this*. So, I got out and danced, mimicking a kangaroo. In complete idiotic abandon, the girl and I were the only ones dancing on a patch of grass surrounded by tables.

When the song finished, the Aussies started shouting, 'Come on over, you Irish bastard. Come and have a drink with us!'

Now, I realised 'Irish bastard' was a compliment, an Aussie term of endearment.

I called Nobby to join us and we started drinking.

The girl I had danced with stuck beside me the whole time.

Her name was Sheila, and she did indeed live and work on a sheep station. She had come to Mataranka with her friend, Congo, who she pointed out to me.

He was sitting on a table about ten metres away, staring at me as if waiting for me to wither. I just stared right back at him, seeing he was of average height with solid shoulders and arms, which I guessed he must have earned wrestling sheep.

Sheila kept asking me questions, but since I was more interested in the beer, the jokes and singing from the Aussie men, she soon would have seen I was ignoring her.

She then went over to Congo and returned, leading him by the hand.

He stood in front of me. 'You insulted my Sheila!'

'I never insult women,' I replied levelly.

'You calling Sheila a liar?'

It was clear where this conversation was going.

After Congo had fired off a sadly predictable insult along the lines of, 'I never knew they piled shite that high,' I decided I'd heard enough, so punched him in the face.

Unimpressed, he swung and connected with a hook to my jaw, then threw more left and right hooks, but I managed to duck them and throw some of my own. Then, I was caught by another blow, this one mightier, winding me and dropping me to my knees.

'That's it. He's had enough now,' said little Nobby, jumping in front of him, but Congo tossed him out of the way as if he was a toy.

Australians loved a fight, and this had all the potential to be a good one, the lofty slim figure from Ireland versus the bulk of their home-grown Congo. They wanted more. Just to make it as authentic an Aussie brawl as possible, somebody poured their cold Castlemaine XXXX down the back of my neck for good measure.

"Come on! What are you waiting for?" He was urging me to fight on.

I got to my feet and Congo looked to finish me off with another wild swing. I felt the air move as it passed my face.

'You're one ugly bastard!' I taunted him. It seemed like just the right thing to say.

Angered, he swung wildly again, and once more, narrowly missed me.

With him off balance, it was my cue to attack.

Torpedoes away! I hit him with my best shot, a straight right landed bang on his nose.

I followed that punch with a rain of blows hard enough to knock out a bear, but apparently, not Congo! Though the fight had started at the tables in front of Wally's stage, because of me backing up all the time, it had made its way down a grassy slope towards the forest and the hot springs. My arms began to drop with exhaustion, a thunderous blow rattling my brain, and everything went black.

The next thing I remembered was an intense feeling of aloneness.

While lying face-up, my eyes opened to a piercing light. A kind of mist, lit up in royal blue, seemed to radiate from my head from a point between my brows. I felt I was leaving my body, floating with great serenity up into the jungle canopy.

***

Looking down at my body and the commotion below, I saw Nobby down there, crouching over my corpse. Nobody could see me and I was obviously dead, simply continuing to float up towards the light.

Eventually, I reached a magnificent golden gate.

An old man was sitting there on a floating armchair, his hand resting on the forehead of an old lady who was hovering before him in a kneeling position.

The old man raised his head. 'This lady is your guardian angel. You are before the Gates of Heaven. Look inside yourself and ask, *am I worthy to enter?*'

The old woman turned, taking a long, intense look at me as if reading my mind. Her eyes, her face, searched mine, waiting. Waiting for what though?

Then as if hit by a pulse of electricity, I knew, joy pulsating through every sinew—figuratively, since I felt like a disembodied ball of energy, a source, a soul.

'Grandma, Grandma, Grandma!' I shouted to her. *'It's me, Paddy ...'*

But I couldn't hear my own voice.

She turned her head back to look at the old man in front of her.

In that instant, I was transported back to my youth, to the time I'd been fishing with my school friend, Anto, at Howth Pier. We weren't catching any fish, so decided to catch seagulls instead. Using a long length of string and two hooks fixed one at each end, we baited both with mackerel, throwing the fish lures to the gulls.

One swiftly caught the bait at one end, a second soon snatching the baited hook on the other. When they flew off, they realised they were bound to one another.

They tried to pull apart as they flew, which we thought was hysterically funny. Normally, of course, the birds would have just continued to fly away, but in my dream, they turned back towards me, squalling and swooping attacking me.

They continued in this frenetic way, their sharp beaks tearing at my head.

I lashed at them with my fists until eventually, they flew off.

The lacerations were painful blood trickled down my face, I looked around, noticing Sean was no longer with me. I was completely alone. Then, people who I had injured in the past, began to appear with hateful faces as if lusting for revenge.

From the depths of my soul, I knew I was not worthy to enter those gates. Terrified, I yelled at the top of my voice, *'I'm sorry for all the wrong things I've done!'*

In an instant, I was back at the gates, that same old man speaking to me.

'Like all human beings, you are living merely to learn, to become wiser, to become worthy to pass through these gates. You must learn to help other beings, rather than fighting and hurting them. Your grandmother has implored me not to look at the man you are now but instead, to give you the chance to prove what you could be in time.

'You are young enough to go back and redeem yourself.'

I awoke in a hospital with a saline drip attached to my arm, a fractured jaw, cracked ribs, and a broken bone in my hand. Nobby was sitting at my bedside.

'Jaysus, Paddy, you know you scared the shite out of me? Thought you were dead!'

'I thought so too.' Then I told him about my experience at the gates of Heaven.

'Wow,' he said. 'They sure gave you a lot of drugs. At any other time, it would have been a good trip but hell …

Anyhow, you must've hallucinated. Are you all right, pal?'

'I don't know, Nobby. Don't think I'll ever be the same. It just felt so real.'

***

Needing rest and recuperation, I wanted to go home to Dublin, Nobby coming with me. I wanted to change, harbouring full intentions to calm down and try to be on good terms with everyone I met from now on. That snippet of a 'life review' up at the pearly gates was serious, showing how many people I had deformed, hurting them physically.

From this moment on, I vowed to avoid all forms of fights by keeping away from places where drunken, loud and aggressive people might be.

I was going to work hard at my career as an engineer and try and find a girl to love.

It was soon after arriving back from Australia that I first caught sight of her walking down the street; I had been looking from the first-floor window of the Georgian building where I worked in Dublin's Fitzwilliam Square.

She seemed so lithe and healthy. Maybe she was an athlete, my mind imagining her lining up to race in the Olympic 100 metres. Where was she from? Not many Irish girls had such dark hair and olive skin. She was probably South American or maybe Spanish or Italian, and she looked to be in her mid-twenties.

She seemed to wield an almost hypnotic power over me. I had no choice but to follow her with my eyes, sure she had no idea she was on stage. *Simply beautiful*, that's how I described her under my breath. She wore sandals and a brightly coloured summer dress, her long, dark hair flowing with the breeze as she walked light-footed along the pavement. I watched until she was out of sight.

She passed by each day at the same time, obviously on her way to work.

I waited and watched for her every day throughout June, July, and August.

When autumn came, I watched her bracing herself against the wind and the rain. Throughout the entirety of the chill winter, I watched her pass, muffled up against the cold. By this time, I was longing to meet her, almost obsessed by the thought.

But how could I make it happen?

February came, and Valentine's Day.

Inside a flower shop, the single red rose in my hand looked so insignificant. Perhaps I should get a dozen. Eventually, I determined that seemed a bit excessive. A dozen red roses would be more appropriate for couples in love. *You don't even know her*, I thought, then settled on a big bunch of early tulips. The lady in the shop assured me my girlfriend would love them.

If only, I thought.

Valentine's Day fell during a cold snap, snow covered the ground with her great white cloak, and frost painted all the trees silver. I stood at the front door of the office and waited until I saw her, trudging through the snow.

Jesus Christ! What are you doing? You don't even know the girl.

Maybe you'll scare her. She'll think she's being stalked!

And maybe she was, though I hoped it was in the nicest possible way, admiring her.

But I had decided to do it, so wasn't turning back. Catching sight of her, I took a breath, walked up to her and said, 'Happy Valentine's Day'.

Between her beanie hat and the scarf that covered her nose and mouth, I could see a pair of brown eyes. Her mittens pulled down the scarf to show a bright smile.

'Are you mistaking me for someone else?' she asked.

'No,' I replied, handing her the flowers. 'I work in that building, and every day since June of last year, I've been watching you walk past in all weathers. I've always wanted to meet you, and today, being Valentine's Day, I thought it might chance it. I lifted my head to look her in the eyes.

'That's kind of strange but kind of nice too,' she said, 'I'm from southern Spain and I really don't like this cold Irish winter, but I do like flowers.

'Which window do you look from?' she asked.

I pointed to it. She looked up to it then back to me, smiled and wished me a happy Valentine's Day. Then she continued walking and I stood relieved.

The next morning, Wednesday, I eagerly waited for her to pass.

When she waved up at me, my heart raced. I waved back frantically and for far too long when I thought about it later.

The morning after that, when she waved, my response was more measured.

On Friday morning, she blew me a kiss.

I sprang from my desk, across the office, down a flight of stairs, out the Georgian front door and hurtled at full speed after her.

'What's your name?' I asked, panting.

'Isabel,' she replied.

'Isabel, could I … take you out to dinner?'

'When?'

'How about tonight?'

We swapped phone numbers, making arrangements to meet later that day.

We had a drink in a Dublin pub before walking to a nearby restaurant, highly commended for its extensive fish menu. I'd already asked what food she liked most.

The conversation flowed freely, getting to know each other over a seafood platter starter for two, then sharing a large, delicious hake served on the bone. We chatted about the cold snap, and she told me she had never seen snow on the ground until now.

I suggested that the Wicklow Mountains were the best place to head to see snow, soon following it up with an offer to take her to my favourite places there.

Furthermore, we needed to do it soon, before all the snow melted.

She told me she had no boots for walking in the mountains, so I offered to pick her up at her apartment to go boot shopping before hiking up the Sugarloaf Mountain.

So smitten with this girl, I would have gone anywhere with her.

***

It was a cold bright day when Isabel and I began our walk from the car park towards the snow-covered mountain, which, rising in the distance, seemed a formidable challenge. Normally, it was a popular hike, but due to these challenging conditions, only a few were braving it that day. We held hands to support each other as we climbed, regaining our breath at the peak, admiring the snowy landscape.

As it was such a bright day, we thought we could make out the silhouette of Wales across the Irish Sea. From there, we drove on to Sally Gap to see a frozen lake in the valley, then let our adventure take us on to Powerscourt Waterfall, where we snapped off icicles and sucked the moisture from them like lollies.

'Are you cold?' I asked, a rhetorical question since I could see—and feel—her shivering next to me, stepping closer to me as if needing my body heat.

She nodded, shivering even more.

I opened my coat and closed it around her shoulders, enveloping her in a bear hug.

'That will help warm you up,' I said.

Once she had thawed, she turned slowly to kiss me, creating a sweet tingle in my lips, its startling sensation rocking me. Pulling back to gather myself, my eyes met hers that were velvet brown, alluring pools. Then we kissed again, again, and again.

For me, that day was the most beautiful ever. A day to cherish for a lifetime.

***

Later that year, on a warm sunny day in July, we took a picnic and went back to Powerscourt Waterfall. There, I took to one knee, asking Isabel to marry me.

She said that our meeting was a dream come true and that she was so happy we would be spending our lives together.

I took a box from my pocket and showed her the diamond engagement ring I had chosen for her.

'If you don't like it, you can change it.'

The ring fitted perfectly.

Needless to say, she had no intention of changing it. Not ever.

'It's so nice,' she said. 'We will be together forever more.'

Chapter 5: Abductions

We married, of course, remaining more than happy, also going on to have four children together.

By this time, three of them were now teenagers: Conan; Hugo; and Ana Marje. Kevin, our youngest, was just twelve. Then, much to our surprise, we got the news that Isabel was pregnant again, and this time with twins. The idea of being a father of twins in my mid-fifties took time to absorb, but as the pregnancy progressed, I warmed to the idea; after all, I'd enjoyed raising the others, so it would give me the chance to repeat the fun. I went around telling the world the great news, but Isabel was worried.

She was now in her mid-forties and the birth of twins often brought complications.

I worked as a piping engineer, specializing in the oil and gas industry which often led to work away from home; back then, I was part of a construction team building a gas terminal in Mayo, in the northwest of Ireland.

It meant I was on site Monday to Friday and since it was a five-hour drive between Dublin and Mayo, there were no guarantees that I would make it back in time if the twins were to arrive early. In fact, it seemed unlikely to manage to make it, but you could be sure that I would be doing my damnedest. Come hell or high water, I'd try.

The children we already had kept us busy, and I was the manager of Kevin's soccer team. One Sunday, I was driving him to play a match when he turned to me, a serious look on his demeanour, and he was pondering on something. Finally, he managed the question, 'Dad, what do you think of all the fat people going missing in America?'

I almost crashed the car, not in shock but because it was so funny. Anyway, it turned out he had seen a report on the news that over in the good ol' U.S. of A., overweight people were ascending into the sky and simply vanishing, never to be seen again.

'*That* was on the news?' I asked in disbelief.

I told him I believed that all events, no matter how strange, eventually had an explanation, and that people didn't just ascend into the sky and vanish.

The explanation seemed to be enough to satisfy him for now, or perhaps he just went quiet because we had neared the

Soon, we were all on the pitch and I was warming up the team of twelve-year-olds. This was to be a semi-final, but all matches were important to the players because every game offered a prize for the Man of the Match, and it was keenly contested.

Children in Mayo rarely drank Coke, Fanta or any of the famous soft drinks. They drank 'Football-Special,' made by a local company, its labelling showing an image of a boy kicking a ball. I brought bottles of it home from Mayo to Dublin each week, awarding a small bottle as the prize.

My team talk went, 'Every boy on this team is special to it. We all know that some of you are better at football than others. That doesn't mean you're not equally important. Every man has to do his job as well as he possibly can. So, this bottle of Football Special isn't for the best player on the pitch—it's for the boy who plays better than he normally does. Now go out there and play as well as you can.'

We were a difficult team to beat since every boy proudly tried his best until the final whistle, and that day, because of it, we won the match. As usual, the team rushed over to me, breathless. 'Who won? Who got the Football Special?' they asked en masse.

I announced the winner and awarded him the bottle. But then I said 'You know what? You were all great. You all worked so hard.'

Then I took two family bottles from my bag for the team to share, and they ran about like mad things as if we had won the World Cup; the 'Football Special' was even better than champagne to those lads that day, big grins all over their faces.

***

Later that day, I insisted that the whole family sat down to Sunday dinner together. 'A family that eats together stays together,' I said—a frequent mantra—as I tucked into roast beef, mountains of mashed potatoes and a double helping of pudding.

All the talk at the table that day was about the curious disappearance of overweight people in the US. Kevin had been right because from the time he had mentioned it, I began noticing that almost every radio and TV news broadcast opened with reports of more cases of obese people ascending into the sky and simply vanishing.

On that day, the news was just full of it.

Distraught family members stood wide-eyed, explaining to reporters how they had watched helplessly as their loved ones just 'floated off into the sky.'

What's next? I thought. *This is absurd! I've heard it all now.* It had to be a hoax. I checked the date—was it April Fool's Day? No, it was the 10th Feb, 2025.

Wouldn't some people just say anything to be the centre of attention? There was no way it could be true and was more likely to be a case of just one person starting something and everyone else jumping on the bandwagon behind them. Or so I believed. It was common enough due to social media.

By the following week, however, what had started in America was now happening in Europe too, reports of vanishings coming from Berlin, Paris, London and Amsterdam. People had hardly finished rejoicing that the Covid pandemic lockdowns had ended, and now, here was another tragedy that managed to be even more bizarre.

Soon, all heavily populated cities of the world had been affected by the phenomenon. The World Health Organization advised that all citizens in the cities concerned should stay indoors, regardless of their weight. It also hastened to assure people that they were safe so long as there was a roof over their heads. That way, something hovering or lurking overhead could not swoop down to claim them.

Probably overcome by the need to be politically correct, so far, no one was daring to give any thoughts for why only the fat were being selected; aside from the tabloids, the media seemed to be avoiding all mention of weight, though the row of photos on the screens made it impossible not to miss the double chins and paunch-laden spare tires.

Our family watched the news together that evening which contained a report from Rome. The College of Cardinals had been summoned to the Vatican. This was followed by a conclave, which was normally only held for the election of a Pope.

After a long consultation, white smoke was seen appearing from the roof of the Sistine Chapel, meaning that agreement had been reached.

The Rapture was upon us, as prophesied in the final book of the Bible, which foretold the ushering in of the final seven years of this age.

True followers of Jesus Christ were being transformed into their spiritual bodies, being snatched up from the Earth to be in Heaven with God. Non-believers were to be left behind to face severe tribulation, the antichrist preparing to take his place.

'Well, I don't know about the rest of you, but I think I would rather take my chances and be left behind than get raptured up to the sky,' I declared, laughing, then announced I was going to bed because of having another early start in the morning.

As I was undressing for bed that night, I saw the reflection of my stomach in the mirror. 'You'd better watch out, tubby, or you'll be joining the ascension yourself.'

I got into bed and fell fast asleep.

***

The alarm went off at 5:00 a.m.

Here we go again, I thought, not looking forward to my five-hour weekly Monday morning drive to Mayo. Although she was still resting and somehow breathing deeply despite the raucous alarm, my hand reached out to gently land upon Isabel's belly. The twins were kicking, and at that moment, I would have given anything to remain there at her side. I kissed her on the cheek, hoping not to wake her, but I did.

She stirred just slightly, dozily telling me to be careful.

I reluctantly got out of bed, got washed and dressed quietly, packed my travel bags and made tea in my travel mug to drink in the car. As I opened the front door of the house, the cold sliced straight through my clothes. It was not even light yet and felt like the middle of the night despite it being a familiar happening. On my way to the car, I ran my work boots over the pavement to test how icy and slippery the roads might be, deciding it was wise to be careful on that particular day.

My tyres gripped the gritted city roads and the motorway, but as soon as I drove onto the un-gritted secondary routes, the vehicle began drifting, making me unable to hold a straight line, driving over a layer of snow with ice underneath.

I could end up in a ditch. What was the point of continuing? If I lost control of the car, at worst, my unborn twins would end up fatherless; at best, I would spend months paying for car repairs. But my engineering team had important work scheduled for the day, so reluctant to let them down and delay the project, I drove on.

County Longford and Roscommon passed in pitch darkness, and as I reached Mayo, dawn began to break. The light of the new day silhouetted the Nephin Beg mountains. As the sun slowly rose, see the snowy caps and rock formations came into view, and in fields below, sheep, the only animals who could survive the cold winter weather.

As I drove slowly and cautiously along the beautiful River Moy, I was transfixed in the presence of the natural world. These views, changing with the seasons on my weekly journeys, made me feel part of the same clay forming this island of Ireland.

After Bangor town, the hills reflected on the calm water of Colene Lake to my left, while to my right, the sky had turned a mysterious red-orange colour, the likes of which I had never seen before. Tthe strangest orange haze hung over an estuary of the Atlantic Ocean. Purple pillars of light and amazing flaming motions pulsated like a heartbeat. I could even see the beams reflecting on the ocean, forming their own glitter paths—the very rare occurrence of the Northern Lights, or Aurora Borealis as it was also known. *What a sight!* I thought.

I pulled the car over, put on my high-vis construction coat, grabbed my phone and started to take photographs. I trudged downhill through a field, scattering the sheep.

Stopping just before the water's edge, I was in awe of the beauty of the scene, lifting my phone to take more photos. Bizarrely, my right hand and arm were surrounded by a yellow glow. Checking, the left had the same aura, so I looked down to my feet. This ethereal glow had enveloped me, and what's more, my feet seemed unable to stay firmly on the ground, becoming lighter, taking on a weird anti-gravity as they commenced pulling away out of the snow, leaving me hovering above ground.

Every fibre of me was in a panic, heart thumping, hands clammy.

Jaysus Christ! What the hell's happening?

'Help! Help!' I screamed out, but only the sheep could hear.

Terrified, I continued floating up from the ground, rising like a hot air balloon. I started praying. 'Our Father, who art in Heaven …' But the nightmare only continued.

As I rose, I could see Belmullet and the Erris Peninsula becoming gradually smaller, feeling enlivened as I was by the sensation of free floating as if in a kid's exciting dream. But this was no dream, and I was no kid. This was real, my breaths catching in my throat, swallowing hard, almost whimpering at the pace of that unwilling ascent.

Despite the thickness of my coat and winter clothes, I got colder and colder, rising higher. My teeth chattered from fear and cold.

Before long, I could see all the northwest of Ireland.

And then I was at the same altitude as an oncoming commercial airliner. As it flashed by, there was a glimpse of the passengers pointing at me from the windows.

I can't survive much longer, I thought as I rose higher still, my breathing becoming heavier and faster. My lungs were burning, my eyes bulging from their sockets.

That's it, I resigned myself. *I'm going to die now; this is where it all ends.*

The face of Isabel swam before my vision, my eyes blurring with tears. The girl—the woman—I loved so much and had won so undeservedly easily, would never know.

Below, the whole shape of Ireland 'floated' and formed, firm on Earth. I was the one floating, the one leaving, headed to a place God only knew where.

Then, surprisingly, my breathing became easier again, and I felt my body warm up. I looked at my hands and noticed that the yellow glow engulfing my body had turned orange. I continued to rise, growing cold again, realising all around was grey. I had left Earth's atmosphere now, reaching the stratosphere. My glowing aura had turned red, making me warm again. *The glow must be protecting me*, I thought, somewhat comforted in continuing to ascend. *Perhaps I won't die after all*.

After what felt like hours, there was no doubt I was in space, able to see the contours of the moon's surface and the sun and stars shining very brightly. Finally, after what seemed like an eternity of cold fear, I somehow managed to turn and look back at the blue-green Earth. *There's no way back*, I thought miserably, gazing around again towards the vastness of the galaxies. And then I saw it, a massive pyramid shape.

It was colourless but reflected the sunlight.

I was moving at increasing speed towards the object, and when I reached the wall of it, a hatch opened, welcoming my body floating toward it as if knowing instinctively where to go, where its true home lay. I instantly entered a chute, the likes of which you would see at a waterpark. The chute sucked me in, feet-first, then shot me along and out through a hole in a wall on the other side. I landed on my back on the floor.

Startled, I scrambled to my feet to discover I was in a curved corridor, not much higher than me, lit up by brilliant, windowless white walls. I felt my heart pounding, drawing in heavy breaths. There, standing before me, were four strange creatures.

I stared, too terrified to move.

They were grey skinned, vaguely humanoid in shape, with elongated bodies and narrow chests. Four pairs of large opaque eyes stared at me, devoid of expression.

As I stared back, searching for some signs of emotion and an indication of their intentions, I noticed their eyes were just orbs without pupils.

Were they hostile or friendly? I couldn't tell. I tried a nervous smile, but no response twitched on their tight little mouths.

They were rubber-stamp copies, about four feet in height, I reckoned, about chest height to me. Their heads looked too large for their bodies and like the rest of their skin, were completely hairless. I could see no ears.

They had no noses either, just two little nostrils where a nose should have been.

We continued to stare, sizing up each other with unblinking eyes.

Then, as if someone had switched them on, they began to move. Their long arms swung loosely, heads turning this way and that. They communicated in chimpanzee-like squeaks and grunts, but their faces were still blank like grey plastic masks.

Then, catching me completely off guard, one leapt up at me and punched my forehead. I reeled from the force of the sharp blow, aware that if those hard skinny knuckles had caught me on the chin, it would have been lights out for me. The next blow was coming, a wild swinging left. I lifted my chin and arched my back, and it missed. I caught the hard elbow as the punch passed and used the creature's momentum to swivel it. I curled my fists—the Paddy of old was back!

'You're one ugly bastard,' I yelled, relying on my old favourite phrase as I landed a right hook. The blow caught it right in the middle of where its nose was not.

Blue pus-like fluid ran down its face, its knees buckling; it slid into a heap on the floor, sending a memory of a familiar thrill pulsing through me.

I didn't see the next blow coming at me. One of the beings swung a red, bucket-like object, catching me on the side of the head. I fell backwards onto the floor, the creature jumping on top of me. Sitting on my chest, it grabbed me by the hair, then lifted my head and rammed it against the floor.

'You overgrown rat!' I shouted, jamming my two fingers into its big glassy eyes.

Its hands shot to its face, and as they did so, I swiped a punch and hit it clean on the jaw. The force knocked it off me and left it lying on its side. I scrambled to my feet and kicked it in the stomach. Turning, I spotted another creature lunging at me and kicked it, full force, between the legs.

What sort of tackle it had, I don't know but it squealed loudly, dropping to its knees before collapsing face first in almost slow motion.

I suddenly felt powerful and in control, but also desperate to get back to my Isabel and the children. Isabel could give birth anytime now, and she would be frantic. I picked up the bucket-looking thing, facing the remaining alien.

'Right!' I roared. 'Tell me how I get out of here!'

It stared back blankly.

'No answer? Maybe this will refresh your memory!'

I swung the bucket and whacked the creature around the head. Its eyes closed, and it slid down the wall to the floor.

'Tell me how!' I yelled at the sprawled bodies, waiting for them to come round. But then, as I watched in despair, all four aliens glowed yellow.

They dissipated, vanishing into a glittering haze.

I was utterly alone. Beginning to be overcome with hopelessness, I sobbed.

In the distance, more chimpanzee noises were audible, and along the curved corridor trotted about ten more of them. These were taller and heavier than the first lot, carrying truncheons in their bony hands.

I lunged forward and kicked the first under the chin with my steel-toed site boots. It fell to its knees, clutching at its throat.

The others pounced, beating me with their truncheons until I sank to the floor.

I covered my head with my arms and assumed the foetal position.

Eventually, I passed out.

Chapter 6: Apparition of the Great Ali

Coming to, I was lying on my back. I tried to sit up and could not, nor could I move my head. A bright light was burning, so to protect my eyes, and in great pain, I struggled to turn away, and in doing so, felt the hair on the back of my scalp tear from the roots. I felt no restraining belts or clamps or anything down along my body.

Maybe my head and clothes had been glued to the stretcher with some sort of special alien adhesive, I thought, still able to move my legs and arms within the confines of my clothes. I could also move my fingers and toes freely, so knew I wasn't paralyzed.

Looking to each side, the area was full of grey creatures, so I closed my eyes, only peeping now and again to check up on what they were doing.

I was one of many humans lying on what looked like hospital trolleys, two handles along the sides of each one. The aliens came in groups of four, collected a trolley and walked two abreast down a corridor with it.

When four of them came for me, I was lying with my eyes closed, pretending to be unconscious though my heart was pounding. They had removed my heavy work coat and boots, but it was still very warm in there. My mouth was dry, and I was terrified.

They walked with my trolley, attaching it to a conveyor belt.

The trolley began to move forward through a tunnel in which bright lights hovered around my body. From the tunnel, the trolley then passed through a scanner which made my whole being tingle and then squirm. I was no longer fixed to the trolley, which tipped up to pour me down a chute. I jammed my elbows to the edge of the chute to stop myself from falling, trying to scramble out.

A Grey saw me and came over, setting about whacking me around the shoulders with his truncheon but I held on regardless, unwilling to be defeated like that.

'I'm going to kill you, you ugly bastard!' I yelled, but it kept beating me.

Tucking in my elbows, I whooshed down the chute, shooting through a hole in a wall and landing on my back on the floor in front of crowds of zombie-like humans.

Back on Earth, if something even vaguely akin to this had happened, it would draw an awestruck crowd and was certain to make the headlines of all the news channels.

Here, my peculiar and ungainly arrival had failed to interest anyone.

After mentally scanning my body for broken bones while the pain of the blows subsided, I got to my feet, glancing around to fully evaluate everything.

The huge space was surrounded by walls which showed scenes of fields and lush meadows, a blue sky with drifting white clouds overhead. I stood on my tiptoes and craned my neck to look out over the sea of grey, balding, human heads.

Right then, I understood what 'Rapture' was.

Humans were being abducted *en masse*.

'That's it, the redemption I got from Grandma it's over. I'm headed for hell! Those overgrown rats are going to pay for this!'

I sank back down against a bulkhead, hanging my head in despair.

'Paddy!' Someone was calling my name from above. 'Paddy, Paddy, Paddy!'

I looked up. Levitating above the ground in front of me was an apparition of Muhammad Ali, bare-chested, standing only in his boxing shorts and gloves, looking as if he had stepped out of the iconic photograph after his triumphant fight with Sonny Liston. A pair of magnificent black wings sprouted from his back.

***

I blinked and rubbed my eyes, hoping the apparition would disappear, but when I opened them again, no such luck. It was still there.

'Paddy,' the vision said, 'You know, you gotta listen! You're now travellin' through the galaxies far from your home with a spaceship full of hostages. God has sent me to be your guardian angel. The heavens are losin' the struggle between good and evil; precious few humans pray to God anymore as you probably know.

'When a person prays, he opens the door to God's love and guidance.'

His wings flexed with his passion.

'Once upon a time, God knew everythin' about everyone an' at that time, the Almighty could more likely provide for them. But not anymore. The internet, as I am sure you know, has taken over. It knows everythin' 'bout a person's thoughts and deeds, can make people believe things that aren't true and desire things of no value.

'But despite his rejection, God still loves his flock, and all the angels wanna help them. God has instructed me to advise and inspire you to lead a human revolt against the extra-terrestrial abductors.'

'*Who?*' I exclaimed. '*Me?* Are you trying to tell me I'm some sort of chosen one? That's crazy. I'm not a leader! I never even captained a rugby team! What do you want me to do, kill all the aliens, take over the spaceship and fly it home? I don't know how to drive a spaceship, and even if I did, I wouldn't know where *home* even was.'

I thought about my words.

'No, I mean I do know where home is—it's where I'd like to be right now! But how to get there from outer space or whatever you call this hellhole, not the faintest idea.'

Muhammed Ali's wings fluttered with impatience.

He voiced, 'I see what you are thinking but *impossible* is just a big word thrown around by small men—men who find it easier to live in the world they've been given rather than explore the power they have to change it! *Impossible* is not a fact—it's an opinion! And *impossible* is but a dare. If your mind can conceive it, an' your heart can believe it, then you *can* achieve it.'

I sighed. Then I had an answer to give to him.

'Muhammad Ali, I'm trying to wrap my mind around the idea that I'm in a hold in a spacecraft and talking to my lifelong hero. My heart is doubting I can lead any kind of human revolt by taking over the ship full of hostages and flying the people home.'

Ali spoke again. 'In April 1967, I was drafted into military service during the Vietnam War. They wanted me to put on a uniform and go ten thousand miles from home on a mission to drop bombs and bullets on brown people.

'The press criticised me as unpatriotic because I wouldn't go, and the New York State Athletic Commission and World Boxing Association suspended my boxing licence and stripped me of my heavyweight boxing title. The US court sentenced me to five years in prison. So, I gave up my title, my wealth, maybe my future.

'Many great men have been tested this way. That was *my* test, and I passed. I came outta' prison stronger than *ever*. The Almighty has chosen you as worthy above all the others for this test. If you accept it, he will bestow on you many talents. And so, it is decreed in Heaven. God rewards with further ability those who *try.*'

That's all well and good, my inner thoughts rampaged, *but what if I* don't *accept it and won't try? What does He have in store for me then?*

I didn't dare to ask.

With that, Muhammad Ali's huge black wings opened, and he ascended through the sky-blue ceiling above and disappeared.

Chapter 7: Cattle Pens

Only partly conscious, my head was telling me this couldn't be reality. On a spaceship, abducted by aliens—was I high and hallucinating? *Maybe doctors have given me some weird medication*, I thought, casting my mind back to my ordeal in Australia. Had I been in an accident? That would also explain why I was hurting all over.

A sharp pain to the shin snapped me to attention.

Looking up, there it was, one of the creatures I had fought earlier. It had just kicked me with a foot that packed the power of a horse's hoof. That kick told me all I needed to know. This was real. This was no dream; it was a living nightmare.

In a vast hall, with moving scenes of country meadows on the walls and fluffy clouds in blue skies above us, stood humans. Thousands of them, mostly male, fat and old. They wore the stinking clothes they had been abducted in and were forming orderly queues, shuffling along towards what looked to be feeding stations.

A Grey looked at me and pointed his baton to the end of one of the queues, so I clambered painfully to my feet and joined it.

No-one glanced at me. No-one spoke. The faces looked exhausted, listless.

Had they been sedated? I tried to talk with an overweight man with long grey hair, but he just looked away. My eyes caught the gaze of an obese, blue-eyed, middle-aged bald man. 'Hey, what's going on?' I asked. But he too looked through me as if he hadn't heard. No-one was showing the slightest bit of interest. *Am I even here?*

I shuffled along with them as they moved aimlessly forward, trying not to breathe in the appalling stench. At the top of the queue, a Grey was scooping pellets into filthy cupped hands. People were lowering their heads to eat directly from cupped hands, avoiding dropping any onto the filthy floor.

At the top of the queue, my hands stretched forward my portion. When had I last eaten? I felt starving. With no fear of what this food might be, I gnawed down into my cupped hands, careful not to drop a single pellet.

They tasted strange, were hard to chew, and dried out my mouth so that I had to peel apart my lips afterwards, a horrible sensation like trying to swallow dry millet or bran.

There was a general movement towards the back of the room, but some people were just standing, bewildered. I pushed past, searching for a bit of elbow space.

In the cramped conditions, the stench of stale unwashed people—and worse—hung thick in the air.

'Good thing our wives can't see us now,' a man's voice muttered to me.

I nodded, that comment bringing thoughts of Isabel to my mind.

Has she realised I haven't arrived at work? Is she out of her mind with worry?

'What's your name?' the man was asking, finally waking me from my daydream. 'Have you just got here?'

I nodded.

He was tall and heavy, wearing a postman's outfit. He held out a big meaty hand and we shook.

'I'm Tom,' he said a little warily, his eyes casting around as if unsure of everything that was going on. 'They lifted me in London about a week ago. Or maybe more.'

'You can't remember when?' I asked.

'There's no way to gauge the passage of time here.' His manner was gentle. 'Are you thirsty, by any chance? Most people are after eating that stuff.'

By *that stuff,* he clearly meant the not-so-delicious and excruciatingly dry food that even a bird would have been hard-pressed to eat. It had left my mouth like a desert.

So, I nodded again, too choked to speak.

Taking me by the elbow, he escorted me to a trough, running the perimeter of the room. I splashed some water on my face, the back of my neck, and then drank some from my cupped hands.

'Help yourself to that shared water whenever you like,' he told me. 'You're treated just like cattle here. You're fed at intervals, you drink water from a trough, and you shit and piss on the floor, then walk in it. No chairs, so we stand or sit in the dirt.'

From then on, Tom and I stuck close to each other, companions in our misery and fear, in a confined and overcrowded space. Most people had nothing to say, but not us as we talked and talked. We compared our scary ascensions. He had been taken on duty while happily cycling down the road on his bike with his delivery of post.

I told him about my own abduction.

Hunger was my closest companion. Whilst awake, I suffered pangs in my stomach, and when I closed my eyes and fell asleep, I had recurring dreams about food. One pellet portion was all I got for what felt like weeks on end. Hunger, anger and missing my family grew like strange bedfellows as the days passed until one day, I could control myself no longer.

In the food line as usual, when I got to the top, a Grey poured pellets into my hands. I ate them quickly, pushing my empty cupped hands towards the alien, begging it to pour me some more. Another Grey saw me, whacking me on the open wrists its baton. It then kicked me behind my right kneecap, sending me sprawling onto the floor into—surprise, surprise—yet more shit. My body stayed there, floundering a while.

As I lay on the ground, it poured pellets onto the excrement.

People watched me slowly get to my feet, making my way alongside the line to the back of the room. As I stumbled along, downtrodden, a song suddenly came into my mind. I started to sing it at the top of my voice.

'When you're weary, feeling small,

When tears are in your eyes, I will dry them all …'

As I sang, people started to quietly join in.

Gradually, more and more joined, our spontaneous choir singing louder and before too long, the entire line was singing. And then, like a Mexican wave, it travelled across the room until the whole space was permeated with the sweet and homely melody.

The song, tune and lyrics alike, seemed to elevate everybody's spirits, the terrible scenario's shared sombre mood lifting.

What was there to sing about? There was always singing when babies were baptised or when a marriage was being celebrated; men sang at work, and soldiers as they marched into battle. Most ominously, there could be singing at and after death.

When I'd finished singing, I clapped my hands over my head.

'Who's going next?'

Then someone else started to sing Hey Jude and we all joined in. After that, another flash choir started from a distant area of the pen, this time giving a rendition of Silent Night, everyone else once more singing along.

When the song was finished, the place fell silent again and my feet shuffled their way back to Tom.

'What do you think is going to happen to us?' I asked him.

'I think we're going to be murdered and eaten—why else would they be taking overweight, mature people? They must be leaving the young humans to propagate the stock, to be eaten later.'

My face must have been quite a picture at that. The primary shock, however, came from never realising or accepting I had let my formerly lean body decline so much that aliens were seeing me as fat enough to render a damn good meal.

'Don't look so surprised, Paddy. Most of God's creatures must do it. Look in the forests and the plains and you'll see species killing other species. Look at humans—we kill just about every animal on land, and we clear the lakes and seas. If they were going to use us to populate some far-off planet, they'd have taken youngsters, wouldn't they?

'So, there are no two ways to look at it. We're going to end up as nuggets and sausages, just the same as the factory-farmed animals back on Earth. Serves us right—well, pardon the pun—because we also call that *food,* not murder ... And now, my friend, what comes around, goes around. It's our turn to be eaten.'

The thought of being taken from my world to somewhere beyond, only to soon be eaten, brought me right back again to my first day of fishing.

***

It was an Irish summer's day, not very hot, under clear blue skies with distant puffs of white cloud. The sea was still, no waves, not a ripple.

The bright sun rose from over the Island called Ireland's Eye, reflecting off the red and white lighthouse of Howth harbour's West Pier.

I sat on the East Pier on a fish crate, looking at the sprat jumping clear of the green water and springing back, trying to avoid the mackerel that hunted in packs below.

It was a perfect day, which I should have been enjoying, but I wasn't. I was filled with jealousy and bitterness. Since early morning, I had been watching other people busily hauling fish from the sea. Other people's fish flapped and jumped and beat against the sides of fish crates borrowed from the trawlers.

I heard fishermen shout, 'There's a shoal in!' as they unhooked mackerel and rushed to get their lines back into the water. Even the seagulls shrieked *ga, ga gawl-ool-la ga, ga* as they perched on trawler rails, on their marks and getting set to swoop down on the scraps of fish discarded by the fishermen during the melee.

I sat alone on a fish crate turned on its side, another empty one beside me standing ready for any fish I might catch. As the day passed, I got more and more frustrated and envious, the only bloke on the pier who had caught nothing. The fishing rod I had received from Mam for my eleventh birthday came with a round, red and white float, six spinning hooks and a heavy weight, all enclosed in hard, clear plastic.

I had tried every spinner individually, convinced they would each catch mackerel, but none did. In my frustration, I tried putting all the spinners on the line, one beneath the other, the float on top and the heavy weight at the bottom. I then cast the line out as far as I could. The float sank a distance below the surface from all the weight.

Other fishermen, seeing the float under the water, shouted, 'Reel in, lad, you've caught a fish.'

So, I reeled in, and when they saw all the tackle on one line, they bent double, laughing at me.

Red-faced, I dropped my head, beads of sweat running from my forehead.

A man on another side of the pier, who had caught lots of fish, put down his rod and came over to me. 'That's not the way you do it, son. Here, I'll show you.'

I watched carefully while the man, with a cigarette between his lips, took a bare hook in his scaly hands and put it on my line above the weight. 'That's paternoster style,' he explained. 'You'll learn how to do it properly; make sure you watch.'

Then he brought over his bait, a mackerel he had caught earlier. He cut a slice from the top of its back to the bottom of its belly and then pushed the hook through the skin side, threading it around the meat and back out through the skin side again.

'That's the way you put bait on, so it won't fall off. An' when you leave the skin showing, the fish are attracted by the shininess of the bait. Try now,' he said, and smiled. The cigarette smoke wafted into his squinting eyes. 'Go on, it's your turn. The only way you'll get it is to keep on practicing.'

He seemed kindly, not just prone to making fun of me. Confident I would now catch a fish, I cast my line and then sat back down on the crate. I held the line against my index finger, able to feel what I thought were crabs pulling at my bait.

I sat for a long time, patiently waiting for a fish, but still caught nothing.

The same man threw yet another struggling mackerel into his box.

He took a Marlboro Red from his packet next, struck a match, and cradling it in his hand, lit the cigarette. Then, emerging from the cloud of smoke that engulfed him, he strolled over to me. 'How come you're not catching anything, son?'

It was a bizarre question; if I'd known the answer, I would have told him. But how could I know why? 'The crabs do keep pulling at my line,' was all that came forth.

'Well, the next time you feel those pesky crabs pulling at your line, you pull back,' he said. 'See how that goes, eh?'

Soon afterwards, I felt one pull at my line. I pulled the rod up in anger, and then the line seemed to head out towards the ocean. *Maybe it's a fish.* The very idea sent a thrill through me. Reeling the line in, my small, light, flexible rod bent in half.

It must be a fish. Can't be anything else, can it? Oh my God!

As quickly as I could, I reeled.

The line was coming towards me, heaving in different directions, and eventually, up from the depths, there it was, the unmistakable silvery sheen. *A mackerel, at last! At last! But hang on ...* I could see another one. I only had one hook on my line, but another fish swam beside it, even breaking the surface and then submerging again when I pulled the hooked one out of the water.

Don't fall off, please don't fall off!

Ratcheting the handle of the beginner's reel, my hand shook, and the fish slowly rose from the water. It bounced off the ten-feet-high granite harbour wall as the line swung from side to side.

I breathed a sigh of relief, observing the mackerel trying to swim on the ground. I caught it in my fist, just below the gills, yanking the hook out of its mouth.

Blood splattered everywhere as I threw it into the crate. Excited, I put on new bait and promptly cast my line to catch another.

It was then that I saw it. I couldn't believe it, nor could the others on the pier.

They pointed, shouted to each other and stared in astonishment.

The other fish had surfaced again and was circling in the water below, appearing to be looking up at me. It was asking me, I'm sure, to throw its friend back in.

For a second, I was tempted, but then thought, *That fish is for Mam's dinner, and I'm keeping it.*

The tail of the mackerel splashed high out of the water before disappearing below the surface. I settled down on the fish crate, looking at the beautiful fish I had caught.

This one was a big mackerel, its oily skin shimmering all sorts of colours, pink gills opening and closing as it struggled to breathe. I watched how it jumped up and down at first, then just flapped its tail as it grew increasingly tired, giving up in the air.

It twitched before eventually lying still.

On the bus home, I thought about that other fish looking up at me, thinking how it must have been wanting me to throw my catch back in again.

I chuckled slightly, thinking, *why, was he your best pal or your brother or something? Your wife? Sorry, buddy. He was far too fat and tasty to throw back!*

At home, I stood beside my mother and watched as, over the sink, she chopped its head and tail off, slit it down the stomach, and pulled the guts out.

The running tap diluted its blood as it ran down the drain.

Then came the delicious sizzle as the fish went into the hot pan.

'Straight from the sea, extra tasty,' she said. 'We'll share it,' she said.

'It's all right, Mam. I don't feel hungry actually,'

***

Back on the alien vessel, I was thinking, standing there among the crowd.

I'm like that mackerel, now.

RED ALERT, RED ALERT!

Those ugly fuckers aren't going to eat me. I'm not going to be dinner for those Greys.

Chapter 8: Rebellion

Standing on my tiptoes, I set off whistling through my fingers to get everybody's attention. A wave of silence swept across the lethargic crowd.

'People, please listen!' I roared. 'I look around me and see a collection of good folks captured and imprisoned! They have wrenched us from our homes, our families, our children. And for what? We don't know, but maybe they're going to eat us. Maybe that's why they've abducted only the overweight folk.'

A collective gasp passed through the group, a crowd in denial about all that extra weight they were carrying around. 'What? You see any thin people here?' I asked.

As for me, I had never seen myself as even bordering on *fat,* only carrying an extra inch compared to this lot. But I had to keep saying 'we' rather than 'you' to make the point, to get them also to accept I wasn't being judgemental. Besides, the aliens obviously did consider me fat, or at least podgy enough to make a decent meal.

This was the plain truth—the plain wobbly, indulgent truth. We all needed to face it.

'Look at us,' I said. 'We're out of shape. All our lives, people have been telling us to lose some weight, slim down, not to eat so much, to get down the gym and work off some of these spare tires. Even our doctors say we have high cholesterol, high blood pressure, a glucose problem ... Who would have thought that they were all right?

'Who would have thought that before too long, our fat would be catching up with us, putting us into this unholy mess? Well, I'm going down fighting. Those Greys will pay with whatever runs through their veins for what they have done.

'Will you fight them with me?' I roared, punching my fist in the air, expecting an enthusiastic, fists-in-the-air roar back. 'We're going to fight, yeah?'

'What for?' someone sheepishly replied from the crowd. 'Even if we won the fight and took over the ship, we still couldn't fly it home.'

'He's an engineer, remember,' one quipped. 'Maybe he thinks he can fly these things.'

'And even if he could fly it, we don't even know where we are!' came another.

Another man shouted, 'Aliens with advanced technology, against ageing fat humans? No! Not me. I'm not fighting anyone. We wouldn't stand a chance.'

'Besides, like you said,' came another from the back, 'We're too out of shape.'

For God's sake, I thought. *Surely, someone will do something! Or are they all going to save their souls by lying down on the griddle and waiting for the heat to rise?*

'Fight and you *may* die,' I agreed. 'Do nothing and you *will* die, or at the very least, you—we—get to live an empty, meaningless life for as long as they decide. And when they finally decide to make a snack out of you in maybe a deep-fat fryer, will you not regret letting those cruel Grey monsters abduct, imprison and eat you?

'Will you not regret never, at least just once, standing up for yourselves?'

Then the words of Muhammad Ali came spontaneously from my mouth. '*Live every day as if it was your last because someday, you're gonna be right.* I'm attacking those Greys next feeding time!' I yelled. 'Who's with me?'

Mumbling came from the crowd.

There wasn't much enthusiasm for the plan initially, but once we got started making weapons, things were changing, spirit bubbling up. A glint was appearing in some of their eyes. We filled socks with keys, coins, or any other hard objects we could lay our hands on, sharing them around. At first, it served to relieve the boredom, then excitement grew until gradually, a spark of fighting spirit came into everybody's eyes.

What happened next would become known as the most notorious rebellion in livestock transportation history. When feeding time arrived, I took the pellets the Grey had just poured into my cupped hand, chewed a mouthful and spat the wet slurry into his face. Grinning at him, I asked for more.

He raised his truncheon, and as he did so, I caught his wrist, grabbed the truncheon from him and delivered a crushing blow to his head. And so began the rebellion.

'Let's kill the bastards!' I screamed, urgently attempting to inspire a frenzy.

A football stadium-like roar rose from our pen, filled to the brim with old, unfit, fat people. With our new weapons, we old fellas fell upon the Greys.

We laid into them, kicking, beating, scratching.

Thousands of wild and heavy, aging humans overcame the guards and charged through the ship, waddling along a luminous orange corridor as wide as a motorway.

As we passed doors on each side, we leaned against them with our shoulders until they burst open, freeing more captives.

There were tens of thousands of podgy humans now freed and on the loose. The badly outnumbered Greys fell to the floor, some men sitting on them, wheezing, all trying to catch our breath. Women gouged at the Greys' eyes with filthy nails.

We all roamed, eyes luminous with anger and hungry for revenge.

I hurried along the corridor, looking for the command centre, but finding only a food store. There, I located more of those same disgusting pellets.

Tom and I were both famished and elated, gorging ourselves on those dried-out granules as if we believed they were sausages. Our progress quickened dramatically, now moving with purpose and forgotten levels of vitality.

Then we literally hit a wall. The corridor was blocked, and we could go no further.

Someone screamed, 'Let's burn this ship to hell!'

Several of our number—it has to be said, of the more moronic variety—tried to set about the vessel with cigarette lighters.

'Stop!' I yelled. 'Are you crazy? You'll kill us all!'

But it was too late. Flames shot up the walls and travelled along the corridor ceiling. We were inhaling toxic gases from the fires, coughing violently.

Many of us were on our knees, holding our throats, choking.

I was sure we were all going to die.

Suddenly, the corridor wall, about one hundred metres away, disappeared to be replaced by a formidable row of Greys.

They had hoses and proceeded to spray a fluid up at the ceiling, spreading down along the walls and onto the floor. Soon, all the flames had been extinguished.

A strong breeze blew from behind the hastily reassembled ranks of our captors. The smoke cleared, allowing us to see and breathe again.

The Greys dropped the hoses to the deck as weapons and shields were passed to the front row from the row behind. Like Roman soldiers, they unsheathed batons and raised them high as they advanced, beating them in marching time against their shields.

I made my way forward to be the first person to face them. Clenching my fist and punching the air above, I turned to our mob, roaring, 'Brothers and sisters! On this day, we will come together as humans to vanquish our alien enemy. One race to fight another. Death or glory!'

Cheering and shouting, we marched slowly together towards the first column. As we increased the pace from a walk to a trot, however, our bare feet found it more and more difficult to keep a steady footing on the slippery, highly polished surface of the alien craft. The fluid they had sprayed made the floor like ice and we slid in all directions.

The slickness did not affect the Greys, their splayed hooves gripping as they marched forward in rows, viciously hewing at us with their batons.

Humans dropped to the floor, unable to fight on what now seemed like an ice rink. They had effectively rendered us as helpless as toddlers or, when we fell, like seals.

Our helplessness did not make them go easy on us by any means, our bones cracking and splintering as they beat us back.

Eventually, we were all separated and dragged back to our pens.

After the thwarted uprising, they punished us by withholding food for the longest time, also turning off the dynamic walls and sky, to leave us in near-complete darkness. No doubt they had conducted much research on our kind, knowing where all our weaknesses and vulnerabilities lay; hunger was one, and the torment of the dark unknown another.

However, despite our suffering, no one among us was regretting our attempted coup, our spirits remaining high and our resolve stronger and more defiant than ever.

From that day onwards, there would be singing and the frequent, rambunctious retelling of all the finest stories of our rebellion. It had been the most exciting, uplifting day, but in the midst of those quieter moments of solitary reflection, we were all resigned to the knowledge that there was no chance of any of us ever getting home.

The exercise of rebelling had been but a momentary respite, but it would not transport us anywhere, least of all to where we most desired to be.

Time passed very slowly. Some people had brought their phones with them when they had ascended but these were useless even before they lost their charge.

People were now—in vain—attempting to keep time with their wrist watches, but without day or night, we had nothing to measure time against. Nobody had any idea of how long they had been on the craft. There were many who also did not wish to know.

Tom and I shared our life stories and must have learnt just about everything there was to know about each other. In his mid-fifties and with young children, we had a lot in common. I told him about my apparitions of Muhammed Ali during my lifetime and back when I had first arrived on board the spaceship.

'These apparitions … they have happened after blows to your head? They might have been a symptom of concussion,' Tom suggested. 'It's common to hallucinate.'

I questioned myself. Of course I didn't know for certain, but I tried to explain.

'Oh, well, I've been bashed on the head many times. The worst occasion being the repeated bouncing of it off the deck of a car ferry.'

'And would you have had an apparition after that?' he asked,

'Yes, to be sure I did.'

So, I told him the story.

***

The requirement to work on the St. Bridget Car Ferry, which sailed from Ireland to France, was that you had to be sixteen years of age.

My uncle worked for Irish Ferries so that rule was overlooked as if it was just incidental, something that no longer mattered if you knew someone who, in turn, knew someone else who just happened to be senior. That way, they could bring in all kinds of visitors who were never supposed to be there on a day pass, let alone for as long as we were allowed to be there. My female cousin and I were both fifteen years old when we worked there for a whole summer season, allowed to work either thirteen or fifteen days in a row and getting either six or eight days off before returning to the ship.

I served full Irish breakfasts for the passengers from 6:30 a.m., finishing the day at 10 p.m. after cleaning up when the canteen closed.

We would then adjourn to the galley mess to guzzle duty-free whiskey and beer. Many of the crew would continue the daily party in their cabins in the bowels of the ship. I wasn't up for that and always managed to sleep, despite the noise.

At 6 a.m. I had to get up to start another day to do the same thing all over again.

People started to notice items going missing from their cabins. The talk was that if the thief was caught, he'd end up overboard.

I was in the galley, shelling pots of boiled eggs, when Declan, a porter, came in. A chef turned to him and asked. 'If ye don't mind me askin', why would ye be wearin' my belt? You do know it's mine, right?'

Declan apologised, saying it had been in his cabin when he had woken up that morning, and since he'd been in a hurry and unable to find his own, he'd put it on.

The discussion made me also eye this lad more closely. The white shirt Declan was wearing looked like one *I* was missing. 'Let me see that shirt,' I said. 'If there's a black ink stain behind your tie, it's mine.' I lifted his tie and there was the black stain.

Before I could loudly accuse him of stealing it, he head-butted me, knocking me backwards. Lifting a pot, he hit me with it, once, twice, three times on the side of my head. Each time, I stumbled backwards then finally, collapsed on my back. He then jumped on me and lifted my head, bashing it repeatedly, against the deck.

Of the people watching the scene, Eoghan, who had escaped political prison in Northern Ireland, knocked Declan off his feet and helped me to mine.

As I came round, Declan was clearly still not satisfied, struggling against constraining hands to assault me again.

'Watch out tonight!' he screamed. 'I'm going to stab you!'

I broke free from the arms around me and charged, grabbing him around the waist in a rugby tackle. I kept running, both of us exploded through the restaurant double doors.

Startled diners witnessed Declan land on his back, with me swinging madly on top.

All the while we were being dragged back into the galley, he continued to make threats to stab me.

Back in the cafeteria, Sean, the grill chef, stared at me.

'How'd you get so roughed up? You all right?' he asked.

'No!' I began to sob. 'Declan beat the shit out of me, and he says he's gonna stab me, tonight.' Tears ran down my face.

'Is he, now?' Sean said. He reached for his meat cleaver and marched to the galley to find Declan. I was later told he grabbed Declan by the hair and pulled his head back, lifted the cleaver above his neck and asked, 'Are you going to stab Paddy tonight?'

He returned to the canteen, gently putting his hand on my shoulder. 'Don't worry, Paddy boy,' he said. 'That Declan is stabbing no one, tonight or any other night.'

Somehow, I believed him though my heart continued its palpitations for hours.

The next day, Declan went on shore leave and when he was due back, I would be going on mine so our paths would not cross for the next two weeks.

His girlfriend, Dervla, worked in the canteen with me. I liked her. We always had a good laugh together. She was eighteen, with straight, jet-black hair, small and skinny—a true, blue, working-class Dubliner.

We'd pretend to be in charge and gave each other orders, then wait for a witty response. One evening, when we were finishing for the day, I told her to mop the deck and then wash all the pots.

She replied, 'I will if you help me feed the captain's cat down in my cabin.'

I had no clue what she was talking about.

I'd heard people talking about feeding the captain's cat, but couldn't even imagine the captain keeping one. Why would he bother? It wasn't as if ships these days were overrun with vermin like in the old days, was it? Wouldn't it just be a liability, something to clean up after and to trip over? And even if he did keep one, why would it make its way down to our cabins for food? I was curious though, so agreed to go.

Dervla drew on her cigarette as we travelled down the five floors in the goods lift. Her eyes seemed to be fixed on me as if contemplating something. She was eighteen, three years my senior, which is a lot when you are fifteen.

'Where's the cat then?' I asked as we entered her cabin.

'I'm the cat,' she said and began to make purring sounds as she rubbed up against me. The scent of her perfume bewitched me.

She then lightly head-butted me and started to nuzzle her face against mine; I felt her soft lips. Nature took its course and before too long, I was in love with Dervla.

We fed the captain's cat at every opportunity afterwards until we took shore leave.

I was in serious trouble because of it, or I would be if ... What would Declan think, or more to the point, what would Declan *do* to me when we met again?

My imagination started working overtime.

He'll surely kill me this time. He'll probably knife me, and I'll die of multiple stab wounds. Or then again, I could just not go back on board. But I do love Dervla, and besides, that would be running away, and Muhammed Ali would never do that.

That's when I had my first hallucination.

I was in the bathroom, brushing my teeth and trying to figure out a solution to my problem when a face appeared in the top corner of the mirror—the face of the great Muhammed Ali. It began talking to me. *'Paddy, he hit you before the bell, he should have been disqualified for that. You must beat him. If your mind can conceive it, and your heart can believe it, then you can achieve it.'*

Then the hallucination was gone.

Most of the crew took an intercity train from Dublin to the car ferry. I meet him again at the train stations platform, I walked straight up to him, said nothing, and hit him before the bell and then as my grandma had instructed kept hitting him. He didn't manage to get on the train.

***

Tom and I soon repeated our discussion of earlier. 'These apparitions ... they've all happened after blows to your head? It does sound to me like they're a symptom of concussion,' Tom suggested. 'And repeated blows will make it easier to occur.'

'Ah, I wouldn't think so. If they were caused by bangs on the head, I would've seen a lot more of the great man, don't you think? Being 6'8" means I was even taller than the frame of a door. I've become accustomed to just ducking under the tops of doorframes, but still I hit my head a lot on low-level chandeliers, signs, cameras, you name it. I have all the scars on my head to prove it!'

I bent down to exhibit my scarred, balding scalp, continuing, 'And there are as many scars on my legs and body from being raked with rugby boot studs. Got a lot of them in London, you know.'

Tom's apparently genuine interest in my story encouraged me to talk more.

'After school, Nobby and I went to college. I managed to get a certificate in civil engineering, and he got a degree in sales and marketing. Since there were no jobs available in Dublin, we went to London. For three years, we shared an apartment, played rugby together, ate and drank together. At that time, the Irish Republican Party were bombing London and the Irish were getting mistrusted and villified.

'We played for London Irish Rugby Club and faced the London rugby teams after the bombings. A lot of the English players we came up against, when they saw our green rugby jerseys, treated it as their opportunity to confront the enemy.

'The captain of our team, Seamus Mullarkey, was a barrister-at-law for the Crown Prosecution Service, a true warrior and captain. He gave a good pre-match team talk.'

Tom raised both brows, eager to hear Mullarkey's wise words.

'It was, "If I could write two things on your brain, it would be *speed* and *ball,* and I'd write it in blood." If the opposition started getting too violent, he'd start throwing punches and wouldn't stop, the team's cue to go all-in. Seamus was a born leader, and we'd follow him like loyal troops into battle. The ensuing thirty-man brawl would inevitably leave the referee with no option but to cancel the game.

'Anyway, during one of these matches, after just five minutes, I got stomped on the shin and then knocked out. Waking up in the dressing room later, I didn't even know what country I was in anymore … I was that disoriented.'

'Was Muhammad Ali in there with you?' Tom asked.

'No, no … that's precisely what I'm saying, you see? If my hallucinations were caused by bangs to the head, reckon I would've had a lot more of them!'

'Go on Paddy, what happened next, then?'

'They brought me to hospital and kept me in overnight for observation. Because I'd been on the pitch for such a short time, I hadn't even got dirty, so they didn't make me shower. Bad error of judgement. This allowed mud, which got under my skin from the stomp, to fester, and a terrible infection set in. I was discharged from that hospital the next day but later in the week I ended up going to another hospital as an outpatient with the infection, every second day at first, then every day until eventually, they had to admit me as an inpatient; the infection had spread, and by now, they were thinking I'd lose my leg.

'They kept me in hospital for three weeks in the end. Three whole weeks!

'After that top-class treatment at London University College Hospital, I was to go home to Dublin and the hospital so kindly helped me by arranging a taxi from the hospital to my apartment to collect my bags then the taxi brought me on to King's Cross Station, where a porter with a wheelchair was to collect me from the taxi and deliver me to the train.

'When I got off the train at Holyhead in Wales, I was to be collected by another porter with a wheelchair who would deliver me onto the car ferry back to Dublin. Nobby had headed home early for Christmas to see his mother, so I was alone. I hopped around with the aid of a crutch, packed my belongings, then got back in the taxi and headed for the station!

'As we pulled in, I spotted a porter with a wheelchair. I hailed him, and he came over and settled me in the chair, my bags on my lap. He introduced himself as Paddy.

'"My name's Paddy too," I said, and we shook hands.

'"You're early for the train. I'll leave you in the bar and collect you in an hour."

'"Good man yourself,"' I said.

'I ordered a well-deserved pint, happy at the thought of being almost home. I reached in my pocket to check my ticket. SHITE, where was it?

'I went through all my pockets, then emptied out my bags. My ticket was gone.

'When the porter returned, I told him I'd lost my ticket but had money to buy another one.

'"No use, Paddy," he said. "It's Christmas and the ferry's full. They can't sell any more tickets—it's a safety issue."

'He then brought me a long way through a series of tunnels to the platform, bypassing ticket inspection, and helped me onto the train. I thanked him and offered him a pile of money for his trouble, but he refused to take it.

'The carriage was an eight-seater, with two facing banquettes. I was the first passenger to arrive, The porter helped me into my seat on the train and to threw my bags in an overhead shelf above. I had it all worked out.

'I'd explain to the inspector that I'd just come out of hospital, that I was on medication and there'd be a porter to collect me in Pembroke.

'I heard laughter. Then a group of Irish lads stumbled onto the train. Some sat in the carriage with me, the rest hanging around the carriage door, drinking from cans. They were all in high spirits, having finished months of labouring; they were now heading home for Christmas with money in their pockets.

'Their clothes were neither expensive nor fashionable. Even with uncharacteristic sums of money in their pockets, they still preferred their tattered clothes and old, worn-out work boots. Their noses were misshapen, and their teeth missing or broken.

'"What happened to you?" one of them asked, noticing my crutch.

'I told him.

'"Here, have a cider," he said, throwing me a can.

'After a while, the ticket inspector came along. The labourers all produced their tickets, but when the inspector asked me for mine, I told him my story.

'He didn't care. If I didn't have a ticket, I was off at the next stop, sob story or not!

'"Listen, square head," a labourer butted in. "Did you not hear the man? He's out of hospital, on medication. His crutches aren't for fun, you know! Says he's being collected at the other end by a porter with a wheelchair. Now why are you going to throw him off the train?"

'"Because I'm the ticket inspector, that's why! It's my job to inspect tickets! And if I can't do that because someone doesn't have one, we have rules. He's off, next stop."

'"Is he now?" the labourer said. "If you come back to this carriage—and I don't care how many square heads you bring with you—one or all of us will throw *you* off the train, head-first through that window there."

'The ticket inspector left and never came back.

'We drank all the cider and thought up a plan. I would pretend to be unconscious when the train pulled into the station. My new labourer friends would then find the porter with the wheelchair, lift me into it and the porter would push me up the gangplank onto the ferry, so nobody would have the opportunity to ask for my ticket.

'It worked perfectly, and we met in the bar to celebrate our success. I shouted a lot of pints on that crossing. I could tell these lads didn't have that much money, after all; it wasn't as things had first appeared. Employed as navvies during the day, when they finished work, it seemed to me from their stories that they were like a band of modern-day medieval knights, living and fighting hand-to-hand in what, in that time of Irish-English history, could sometimes be a hostile, foreign land.

'My father was there to collect me off the boat. He looked so alarmed to see me in that state, drunk with all these the hardy looking navvies.

'"These your London friends, lad?" he asked me.

'I told him they hadn't been, but they sure were now. I pulled myself together to act somewhat sober as Mother would be anxiously waiting with a big roast dinner ready.

'It took a while for my leg to heal, so I had to quit my job in London. Nobby went back alone but didn't enjoy it without me, so moved back to Dublin soon afterwards.

'We got jobs, played rugby and drank in the local bars. We lived happily in Dublin for about two years, and then, one Sunday night, we bumped into an old friend, Podge, in The Castle pub. He was just back from Australia and full of the joys of life.

'He had great stories to tell, and by the end of the night, Nobby and I had caught the wanderlust and so, that's what set us on the path to Australia.'

'You mean that's where you had *apparitions* of your grandmother and St. Peter after you got thumped,' Tom interjected like a stuck record. 'Listen, like I keep saying, they've all happened after blows to your head. They're symptoms of concussion. You're inflating them big time into something they're not.'

Tom seemed more and more convinced about the concussion, but still he was listening, rapt, like a group of little kids engrossed in a fairy tale. His eyes were wide.

Suddenly, a wide beam of light appeared high on one of the darkened walls, the brightness spreading vertically as a rush of fresh air filled the space.

And then I saw blue sky, *real* blue sky, not an artificial backdrop. It was like daylight peeping through the curtains after a long, dark night. I beamed with joy. Those of us who were awake roused the others, all shielding our eyes as we gazed towards the opening. Then, the whole wall slid sideways, revealing a yellow sun.

Our lungs filled with the sweetest scent of authentic Earth-like country air. We looked at each other in amazement.

Smiles and nervous laughter were breaking out all around.

'What next?' Tom asked, blinking at this sudden brightness.

Chapter 9: Planet Diaz

We made our way forward, clinging onto each other as we shuffled down a ramp into a world with green trees, giant multi-coloured mushrooms and green meadows. A myriad of rainbows coloured the sky. We had landed without realising it.

Greys stood at each side of the ramp, ensuring there was no possibility of making a run for it. From the ramp, we were carefully herded into a fenced marshalling area.

As I looked around, trying to work out what was happening, a rope shot through the air, fell over my head, and slid down around my arms.

I had been lassoed. Two Greys clasped onto the end of the rope, two more setting about me, kicking at the back of my knees to take me down.

The other two were tugging on the rope until I lost my footing.

Tom tried desperately to intervene, but a baton blow to his head must have reminded him that resistance was futile. Now I was on my knees, one Grey grabbed my hair, another holding my head while mercilessly prodding a device into my ear.

Suddenly, to my amazement, I heard a simultaneous translation of what they were saying, understanding every command.

'Don't move! Stay still!' one barked, using its long, cold fingers to attach a halter with a throat band to my head. A ring dangled from the halter, connected to a leash.

At the end of a leash I was dragged to a building. Inside was a long corridor, cells on each side, each just large enough to fit one human, standing.

The Grey nudged me into a cell, detached my leash, closed a gate, and left me alone.

Once the sound of its steps left the corridor, I could hear that I was alone.

The cell did not even afford me the space to turn around, but why had I been singled out? My bare feet throbbed and burned against a hard serrated floor.

The day was hot and humid, exhausting me just to stand and to try and catch my breath. As I panted, long rivulets of sweat were running down from my forehead into my eyes. I longed for water. How long would they keep me here?

Maybe for the rest of my life. I might die from thirst.

Then, I heard the welcome sound of footsteps.

As I poked my head out through an opening in the barred gate, my eyes could not believe the sight: two miniature, human-shaped creatures walked towards me. The smaller, one I guessed to be a child and scarcely higher than my knee, was tugging a man along by the hand. He was head and shoulders above her, making me easily assume he was her father. When they reached my cell, she stopped to point at me.

'I want that one!' She said it as if choosing candy in a store window.

She stared straight up at me with shining eyes, and I stared back. There was something oddly familiar about both of them. The child wore a green dress and red cape, held together with a brooch. The tiny man beside her possessed bushy sideburns, a full curly beard and a red nose. But what I found most striking was his green top hat with a black buckled belt wrapped around it and a gold-buttoned green velvety jacket.

I blinked again. *Jaysus Christ Almighty, Mary, Joseph, and all the saints!*

If I'm not mistaken, these are leprechauns!

He even carried a wooden fighting cudgel, recognisable as an Irish *shillelagh*.

I must be hallucinating, please let me be hallucinating again.

This is all too much. Wake up, Paddy. Wake up!

But I didn't.

The girl jumped up and down with excitement. 'Dad! Dad! Dad!' her translated voice squeaked in my ear, and some words sounded vaguely familiar. They were speaking Irish, a language I'd stubbornly refused to learn in school, thinking it was dead and I'd never have the need or opportunity to speak it. So, I barely knew a word. It was as strange to me as they were, yet weirdly comforting to hear at the same time.

'I want that one, Dad! Dad! Dad! I want that one!'

The father wanted to keep moving. He tugged at her hand, but she held her ground.

'Lal, that's typical of you!' he said. 'Not only do you want a Nayzic, but you want the biggest one I have ever seen. Just look at the size of it!' His voice went up and down melodically, like listening to singing as he spoke. 'How would we ever feed it? Besides, the suburbs are no place for a pet. They need countryside.'

'But you said I could have one! All the girls in my class have one!'

She looked as if she might cry.

Her father's pointed ears waggled. 'Lal, we simply can't afford it.'

'Dad, we've been through this before!'

I followed this conversation, wondering which way it would go. I liked the idea of being bought and freed from this prison, taken home to be cared for.

'Now, Dad,' said this foot-high child, fiddling with her broach. 'I told you, I've got it all worked out. For money, I'll charge the other children to have rides on its back.'

Her father knitted his bushy eyebrows.

'Dad!' the girl pleaded. 'I love it—look at its eyes and its big nose and look how huge it is.'

So, they intended to use me as a pony?

At least it sounded as if I'd be cherished and fed.

Her Dad sighed. He opened the buttons of his jacket and took out a polished golden flask which he lifted to his lips, and from which took a swig.

'*Please!*' came the high voice in my ear.

'But what if that Nayzic is wicked?' the little father said. 'What would we do then?'

'Dad, it's a *male*. A girl in my class had a wicked male Nayzic. Her parents sent for the vet who threatened to cut its balls off, and it was never bold after that.'

I'd behave, I decided.

No matter what objection her father raised, Lal seemed to have a clever counter- argument. It continued in this fashion as they moved farther down the corridor.

I waited in that cell, hot and thirsty for some time, until a Grey returned, attached a leash to my neck and led me back outside. In the distance were leprechauns, mounted on Greys' backs, herding groups of humans.

There were so many, I'd have little chance of ever seeing Tom again.

Impatiently, the Grey dragged me by the throat band until we got to a small parade ring. There, I was to be auctioned, I realised. The mart was surrounded by loud, laughing, drunken leprechauns. I didn't much like the look of them, nor the smell of whiskey and general foulness on their collective breath. I hoped the girl would buy me.

The bidding started.

Then that familiar shrill voice piped up in my ear.

'Dad, Dad, I want that one! Dad, Dad, Dad I want that one! Dad, Dad, Dad …!'

It was so incessant that some of the other bidders started to copy her. *Dad, Dad, Dad, I want that one! Dad, Dad, Dad, I want that one! Dad, Dad, Dad! That one!*

Her father made the first bid.

A drunk shouted to him, 'Tell your cailin to hold her gob with her wailing so we can do our business!'

'Arrah, shut your gob,' the father shouted back, lifting his stick.

Shillelagh law meant it was customary to let out rage, so it looked like a row and ruction would soon begin. Attempting to distract from the melee, the auctioneer raised his hand. 'Sold to Maistir Rafferty and the cailin in the green dress and red cape.'

A disgruntled bidder threw a bucket of whiskey punch over the hapless auctioneer.

I was led from the parade ring to a holding area where the little girl and her father joined me.

'Dad, it's a lovely Nayzic, and you got it at *such* a good price—you're the best Dad ever. But the poor thing, look at it. It's very droopy. Maybe it's thirsty.'

Yes, yes! I said inwardly, wondering if she understood.

She lifted a bucket of water up to me in her tiny hands.

I smiled and nodded, took the water from her and guzzled it noisily.

Delighted, she then ripped off the corner of a big sachet and handed it to me.

I squeezed some onto my tongue. It tasted like the tomato sauce you would get in sachets from fast-food restaurants. I squeezed it all into my mouth, waiting for it to reach my empty, howling stomach.

Lal sniffed me. 'Ooooh,' she said, holding her nose. 'There's a smell of sewer coming off it! Its hair's all stuck together as well, and it looks like it rolled in poo. We'd better wash it before we bring it home.'

With my head in the halter and the leash in her hands, she led me into a pool of smelly, cold disinfectant and left me to splash around for a while.

I ducked my head under the water. It was luxurious. And after I was done, I was led into another pool which smelt of perfume. When I came out, a stretchy pair of leggings and a tee shirt were waiting for me, as well as socks with thick outdoor soles.

I was clean, no longer thirsty or starving hungry, and I was alive. I spoke clearly, telling them how happy I was to have been bought by them, but the words obviously made no sense. They made no response or even a sign they had heard me.

Lal could hardly keep from stroking and patting me with her tiny hands.

I was aware of more leprechauns gathering around me below my waist. They appeared to be marvelling at my size.

'He's the most beautiful Nayzic I have ever seen,' said a tiny auld leprechaun woman, sitting in a rocking chair and smoking a pipe. 'What're you going to call it?'

'Misty,' said Lal and the heads bobbed up and down.

It was a lovely name, they agreed, and would suit me.

Lal proudly led me away, her very own Nayzic.

I followed her with something like contentment.

I could have done a lot worse, happy to be alive but determined to get home to my family, nothing was going to stop me.

She led me to their transporter, a vehicle with windows and doors like an Earth car, but without wheels. The two leprechauns sat along a front seat, and I curled up on a blanket in the back, my head close to their seat, feet sticking out of the rear window.

The vehicle took off soundlessly, floating above the ground.

Nobody guided it; it just seemed to know the way.

I looked out of the window of the craft as it skimmed through grassy meadows and soared over forests and lakes. *This is not too unlike Earth*, I thought, attempting to listen in to their conversation.

'What are the people going to do with those Nayzics they bought?' Lal asked.

'Well, some will be pets, like yours,' he said. 'Some will work the farms, and the rest will be eaten.' He said it without a hint of emotion.

'*What!?*' Her tiny nose wrinkled. 'Who would eat a Nayzic? They're so lovely!'

'Well, *you* for one!' His rosy cheeks glistened as he grinned. 'What do you think they sell at the supermarket? What do you think that meat is, all nicely cut and packaged?'

'Ah, Dad, did you really have to tell me that? That's horrible. I swear I'll never eat Nayzic again. I'm going to become a *Gan Fheoil* a vegetarian! Anyway, why don't Gan Fheoils eat meat?' she asked. 'And why do they live on a different continent?'

As I lay there, still not quite believing what was happening, I listened to her dad tell the following story.

'Many generations ago, people began to question if it was right to breed farmed animals. Many believed it to be cruel, and others were concerned that gas from their dung was causing global warming. A referendum was held, asking whether eating meat should be banned. The *Right to Choose to Eat Farmed Meat,* the Do Rogha party, easily won but agreed that the breeding of animals on Diaz would have to stop.

'So, the De Roghas travelled through the galaxies to bring home many different species of animals from many other planets to eat but inadvertently, they brought back a species that looked uncomfortably similar to us. The Gan Fheoils were horrified to see them hanging from butchers' shop hooks, demanding a stop to importation.

'Tension grew, families becoming bitterly divided to a point where they would not eat at the same table. What were intended to be peaceful street demonstrations turned into bloody, pitched battles between the factions. States took sides, then countries, and soon, the whole planet was at war. The Do Rogha, the stronger side, forced the vegetable eaters out to a smaller continent across the sea, now known as Gan Fheoil.'

'Wow, Dad! *I* would've become Gan Fheoil too! So, how come we eat meat?'

'You have been raised a Firinne Nadur which is a belief allowing meat to be eaten sparingly, and then only from animals that have lived a full, natural life.'

'Explain what that means?' the girl urged.

'There once was a beautiful pond surrounded by flowers and shrubs with lilies floating on the surface of the water. It had, however, no fish living in it. So, the owner stocked it with rainbow fish, and visitors to the lake now had something else to admire—colourful rainbows leaping out of the pond to catch flies in mid-air. Well-fed on flies, these fish multiplied, and the pond became full.

'Anglers noticed the abundance of fish, so they decided to catch some.

'The hooked rainbows fought bravely for their lives, dashing to and fro, thrashing about in the water and leaping high in the air to rid themselves of the nasty hooks catching in their mouths. When they were landed, their bleeding gills opened and closed as they gasped for breath. They writhed at first, flapping their tails, and the nerves in their bodies twitched violently before they eventually died.

'Visitors, watching this scene, were outraged by the cruelty and persuaded the owner of the pond to ban fishing. With angling banned, the fish had no predators.

'So, the rainbows continued to multiply until there weren't enough flies to nourish them. They began to starve. Weakened, the fish became diseased, a state which spread throughout the pond, and they all died. Now, the Firinne Nadur believe that had the anglers been allowed to catch and eat the larger fish, then the rainbows, flies and anglers could have lived in balance. You see, Lal, you can't cheat nature and the longer you do, the worse the consequences will be when mother nature comes to call.

'You see, sooner or later, she comes for her redress. It's called payback.'

In the back seat of that vehicle, I was torn between gazing out of the window at leprechauns working in the fields, at the strange plants, animals and the many rainbows in the sky, and listening to this fascinating parable. For now, the parable won.

'The planet is like the pond, and just as the pond could only sustain so many fish, the planet can only sustain so many Diazians. There must be enough space left for all of nature too,' he said as he glanced out of the window.

The transporter hovered and landed in a square field of green.

The back door opened automatically.

I straightened out my legs and pushed myself out, my feet landing onto spongy moss as I looked around with wide eyes.

On one side of the square was a giant yellow mushroom with blue and red flowers blossoming on top. Detached cylindrical shapes lined the other three sides of the square. *These must be homes,* I concluded.

Lal led me around the back of one of the homes and into a shed. 'Here we are, Misty,' she said, opening the door. 'This is your new home.' She laid out a mattress on the floor. 'Lie down and be a good boy, go on.'

I obeyed, and Lal spread a blanket over me and left.

I heard her bolt the door behind me.

Hinged doors, bolts ... I had arrived by means of an intergalactic spacecraft into a land that seemed not much more technologically developed than Earth. It didn't make any sense. I lay on the mattress in my new clothes and pulled the blanket to my chin.

I was already feeling cold, and the halter sat uncomfortably around my head. Wrestling it off did not work as the damned thing would not even work loose.

I was beginning to doze from the exhaustion of the whole experience when I heard the bolt slide.

The door opened again. It was dark outside, but the light from their home illuminated the shed. Lal had returned with another blanket, a container of water and two sachets of food. 'Aaaah, I bet you're hungry?' she said.

She snipped the top off the first sachet.

When I had finished, I drank more water, and Lal took off my halter.

What a blessed relief. 'Time to sleep,' she said.

I pulled the two blankets back over me, feeling warm and clean then, and my stomach was full, a sensation not known for some time.

Lal wished me good night.

She seemed very nice, I had arrived at a good place, a place which I planned to escape from.

Chapter 10: My Life as a Nayzic

I awoke in the morning to the door opening and the sun shining into my eyes.

Lal was with a boy in a green top hat with a gold buckle similar to her father's, also a green jacket with black lapels and gold trim, black trousers and shiny black shoes, also buckled to match his hat. She introduced him to me as her brother, Cahir.

He had the same pudgy, happy features as his father but on a younger, fresher face and minus the bushes of hair sprouting from his father's ears. He stood watching curiously while I ate the welcome breakfast sachet Lal had brought me.

She passed me up another, which slid down quickly.

I had a lot of eating to catch up on.

When I had finished, she asked me to get down on my hands and knees.

I didn't want that halter on my head again, so didn't budge.

Then she got down herself to show me what to do.

It then occurred to me: they didn't realise I could understand what they were saying, but if I didn't obey her commands, I could easily end up back at the parade ring.

I obliged so she could put the halter on.

She produced a cane basket with straps that slipped over my shoulders like on a grape-picker. Then, she tightened them.

If they thought I was just a dumb beast of burden, it would make my escape easier when the time came.

'You're a very good Nayzic,' Lal said, stroking my long hair and beard.

Then this tiny girl gestured to me to stand up and led me by a leash to the square green in front of the house, the same spot where we had arrived in the transporter.

Word travelled quickly that I was on show. Leprechauns came pouring out of their homes to see me and roared at my size.

'It's as tall as the top windows of my house!' one laughed.

'That one's going to take a lot of feeding!' observed another.

'I hope you're ready to clean up after it!'

Lal tapped me lightly on the knees with a small cane, pulling on the rein of my halter, saying, 'Down, down, boy!'

I dropped to my knees.

Then, Lal put her foot in her brother's cupped hands, and he boosted her up into the basket.

The gentle tap on the neck was presumably an order to start moving, so I began to walk forward. At another tap and an instruction to 'go on', I began to jog, and at another, broke into a run. I could hear cries of joyous, raucous laughter as I went through the routines. It felt good too, my spirit feeling oddly liberated.

When we were halfway around the green, her brother Cahir called that it was his turn. Soon, all their delighted friends had been for a short round. When I had finished, they gathered around, complimenting Lal on her choice of Nayzic.

Lal then announced that I would be down on the beach the following day. 'If anybody else wants to ride my Misty, though, they will have to pay. The money,' she added, 'will go to a good cause—feeding and looking after me. Like you said, it's expensive. He's already been through two whole feed sachets.'

Murmurs passed around, but no one seemed to object to what she was suggesting. Everyone leaned forward again, peering, taking a last look at the Nayzic.

Then Lal led me to the back garden for a much-needed rest. Or so I hoped.

In fact, throughout the remainder of that day, a stream of the children's friends came around to see me. Each patted me and brought me sachets.

I luxuriated in the garden sunshine, dozing and eating, a far more comfortable existence compared with that dark, dirty, stinking pen I had come from.

Just before dusk, Lal put me back into the shed for the night.

***

When I awoke the next morning, I felt fresh and reinvigorated, curious about my upcoming visit to the beach.

We walked at a slow, leisurely pace through a multi-coloured forest, taking in the wonder and beauty of the nature all around us. It was invigorating to breathe in a deep lungful of the scent of the trees, the giant mushrooms and the flowers.

The canopy opened out to a sandy beach and a beautiful ocean, blowing a light, salty breeze onto my face.

Many excited leprechaun children appeared to be waiting impatiently for my arrival.

'Roll up to ride the tallest Nayzic on the Planet Diaz!' Lal announced. 'Only two gead for five minutes and five for fifteen minutes. Walking only.'

Cahir organised a queue which grew longer and longer.

The Diazians and the basket on my back weren't heavy, but after a morning of plodding my way through soft white sand, my feet were dragging. Panting and sweating, I was exhausted and badly needing a break.

Lal gave me water but no food, not this time. 'I think Misty is starving,' Lal said to Cahir. 'Look how skinny he is. I'm going to give him more to eat.'

She snipped open a sachet, and when she handed it to me, I devoured it in one gulp.

'But he still looks hungry, doesn't he?'

'He does, Lal,' said Cahir. 'Give him another two and let him rest a while'.

I devoured the next two, and as soon as I had rested, volunteered to continue carrying kids up and down the beach.

Completely out of condition, I soon tired again.

Cahir noticed me dragging my feet. 'That's it for the day. You're all wearing him out. He still has to get used to being here; you don't want to make him sick.'

So, that was indeed that; no more children were permitted to join the queue. Finally, at the end of a very hard day, I was led back to the house by the leash.

The children's father had just finished the job of cutting a hatch high in the shed door so I could look out of the top.

'How did you get on today? Did you make any money?' he asked.

'In rides, about two hundred gead. A sachet costs five gead, so if I feed him five sachets a day, that's enough for eight days.'

'That's my Lal!' he said. 'You're a little star. There's no stopping you. But why five sachets? I thought two would be enough.'

'He's a very big Nayzic, and I don't think he's been fed properly for a long time. I'm going to wash him now; he is very smelly again.'

I crouched on all fours while she washed me down. Stripped of my clothes, I was enjoying the cold water being hosed all down the back of my neck and head. After such an exhausting day, the pampering was delightful.

As she soaped the rest of my body, I heard her repeated gasps.

'Dad, Cahir, come quickly! Look at the scars and bruises on him. I think this Nayzic must have been beaten on the transport ship.' She bunched her little fists. 'All animals should be treated fairly, no matter how stupid we think they are. Dad, you must find out who beat Misty and get them dealt with.'

He sighed. 'Lal, who exactly do you think I am? With all the transport ships in the galaxies, how do you expect me to even find the one that brought this Nayzic here?'

'I don't know,' she replied, her mouth downturned. 'But try your best, won't you?'

***

Her father found out, and I was there when he told her what he knew.

'A riot broke out when one of the Nayzics asked for more food. When the Grey would not give him any more to eat, the Grey received several blows to the head from the Nayzic. This gave all the Nayzics confidence and incited them to stampede. I'm told many Greys were killed and injured in the melee.'

'Well,' Lal said, gazing at me in adoration, 'He had nothing to do with that. He's too nice. My Misty Moo-Moo would *never* be involved in a riot. Sounds silly to me.'

I put on an innocent face.

Just like the humans back on Earth, Lal was already besotted with her pet.

At first, it seemed I was with a happy family, but sometimes, when I lay in the garden, there seemed to be a disturbance in the house. Shouting matches, banging noises, and crying. After one such commotion, Lal came running out of the back door and sat on the doorstep with tears running down her face.

I crawled up to her on all fours, looking lovingly into her eyes.

Then I rested one hand lightly on her knee.

'I miss my mother,' she said between sobs. And then it all poured out. Her mother had recently left, seeking "laughter and whatever another life would bring."

I tilted my head to show how well I was listening, trying to be a friend.

'I'll never stop missing her,' Lal said, wiping her eyes on her sleeve, though still sniffling now and then. She suddenly cheered up, dimples coming to her cheeks. 'But I have you now, Misty-Moo! Come indoors, let's see what we can find you to eat.'

Later, she made me up a bed, and I could barely believe this one was to be indoors.

Living in the house now, I soon saw how the family had been broken by their loss. While the children went off to school, their dad stayed at home.

He talked to me as if I was some dumb animal, complaining about how he missed his wife and daytime job and felt completely useless as a stay-at-home Dad.

He had bought me only because he thought a pet would be good for the children's mental health. Surely, I helped with his too.

I was always ready to snuggle up next to them and make them feel less lonely when they wept at their loss. Sometimes, the anxiety and stress boiled over, however, manifesting in the outbreak of terrible fights and one or two random flying objects.

Somehow, it was usually possible to wordlessly intervene, sometimes by deliberately positioning myself in the firing line. On other occasions, it seemed as if my very presence in the room wielded a calming influence on the family.

I was a useful distraction to them, aiding them to avoid constantly dwelling on their unhappiness. There was more to think about than misery and woe, so each time either of them was sad, I would edge up, nudging them with my nose or a hand.

It seemed to help, making them smile and laugh.

'You are such a funny one,' Lal said to me quite often. 'I am so lucky to have you.'

Not only did they feed me and give me affection, but I also served the purpose of an unofficial therapist, albeit a mute one. In short, I had become part of the family. They had even started feeding me from the table by now.

Despite trying to avoid their meat, when the aromas came wafting right up my nose, I had to keep swallowing to stop myself drooling. I dreaded to think what that meat was.

For their part, the family took very seriously their responsibility to care for me. Each weekend, while their friends lay around deciding whether to get up or not, they rose early and sold rides at the beach, taking ownership of the task of getting money for my food. It built a great bond between them and helped them develop high self-esteem.

It brought structure to their day, and they slept well at night.

I lived there for a long time. It seemed there were no winters and summers there to mark the years, the sky full of rainbows every morning, the sun shining every day, and then it would rain for the same duration each night as if by clockwork.

The family's grief and anxiety eventually passed.

I was loved so much and treated so well I could not bring myself to do anything to upset them. Yet every night before I slept, there was one thing I had to do, to pray to the Almighty that I would one day get back to Earth. I did this in the knowledge, of course, that there was no possibility of this ever happening. My heart had given up.

Since arriving in Diaz, I had spent up to whole days in the back garden, having only ever seen the beach, the public park and the green in front of the house.

The father would never ride on my back, but he took me out for a walk once or even twice every day without fail as if he drew something therapeutic from it.

Of the three spots we frequented, the beach was my favourite place.

From a pier, he threw sticks into the water. I swam to retrieve them, returning them to him to throw again.

The Diazians watched me and cheered as I came out of the water. They waded in themselves to cool off but were heavy little creatures, all unable to swim.

The father always spoke to me as we walked, making me deduce he must have needed somebody to confide in. There was worry all over his face the day he told me he was sinking into debt because he wasn't working, and many bills had not been paid.

He looked at me sadly. 'Something's got to go; it's either you or the transporter. I may need the transporter if I get a new job, but I wouldn't like to face the children if I sold you. So, Misty Moo Moo, you are not going to the meat factory just yet.'

My heart drummed in my chest at the awareness of the dilemma and narrow escape.

Lal was angry when she heard the transporter had been sold. 'All my friends' parents have transporters! Some even have two. How come we won't even have one?'

Once he'd explained it was either the transporter or me, Lal became quiet.

To that, it seemed she had nothing whatsoever to say, and she simply shrugged.

Time passed and Dad was still out of work. But he wasn't home the day the sheriff and his assistant called. I was in the garden, sitting with Lal and Cahir.

The sheriff produced a warrant to remove the family's possessions, and he deemed me the most expensive item in the house. He apologised as he went to get my halter, saying it was just his job. If they were fortunate, he added, they might come into some money and might still be able to obtain me back at a premium. *If* I hadn't been sold.

I watched the tears welling up in little Lal's eyes.

'Please don't take my Nayzic,' she pleaded. 'Please. He's mine. I'm a child, and children can't have debts.'

It seemed she knew all about the law, even at such a tender age. But it did not help because my ownership had been written in her father's name, a terrible mistake.

I had to come to her defence, the anger boiling up in my veins. I sprang to my feet, took a deep breath and snarled out through clenched teeth, 'Don't upset the children!'

Nobody understood a word I was saying, of course, but the sheriff must have grasped the point when my fist came slamming down on top of his head.

Picking up the halter he had dropped, I fiercely lashed his assistant with it.

'Stop that Nayzic, or I'll shoot him,' growled the sheriff. He was back on his knees and pointing a gun at me.

Lal was screaming for me to stop as the tears rolled freely down her cheeks.

Cahir leapt forward between me and the sheriff.

'Then you'll have to shoot me first,' he said. 'He's one of our family.'

The Sheriff lowered his weapon upon realising my struggling had ceased.

'That's one mean Nayzic you have there. But like you said yourself, young lady, you know the law. And the laws state that any Nayzic beyond a juvenile that assaults an officer must be put down. I'll be back tomorrow to take him away,' he said en route out.

After much deep breathing all around, things became calmer.

Lal then started to cry. 'Misty's going to end up in the meat factory, and there's nothing we can do!'

Cahir was pale and shaking, 'No, he's not. We'll set him free.'

'Where?' asked Lal. 'You know he will be caught.'

'Well, you know how on a clear day you can see the silhouette of Gan Fheoil from the beach?'

Lal nodded.

'They don't eat meat there. Misty's a good swimmer. We'll point him towards it, and he can swim there. I know we don't want to have to let him go and say goodbye to him, but Misty will surely be killed and eaten if we do not act quickly. We have to act, honey.'

***

They brought to a deserted beach at the very first light.

The siblings wept, knowing they were feeding me for the last time. They pushed some sachets into my leggings' pockets, patting my head a hundred times or more.

I had grown to love this family, and part of my heart would always be with them. A whim of fated had decreed that we were to be separated by my death or distance, and forever. And as painful as those feelings were, I let myself feel them, realising how much we had given to each other. I lifted them up to my chest and hugged them.

They wrapped their arms around my neck, sobbing and clinging to me desperately.

In time, I let them down, keeping my stretchy top and leggings on, but taking off my socks with thick outdoor soles and looking out at the sea.

None of this is fair. I'll survive, though. Like I always do. I just need to be strong.

I began wading into the freezing water, seeing nothing but the horizon in front of me. When the water reached my waist, I looked back to the shore.

'Swim, Misty, swim!' the children cried. 'You have no chance here. We love you! Goodbye!'

Off I swam, allowing my body to be borne away by the waves and lost in the distance, the children did not know where I had come from or where I was going to.

Chapter 11: Vegan Hospitality

I swam steadily as far as I could, and then stopped, exhausted, floating on my back for a rest. There was no heat left in my body, the cold water reaching into my bones.

The sea grew rough, with large deeply undulating swells.

As I looked forward, all I could see was a wall of waves. At first, I managed to float over the wall but then began to go under, swallowing great gasping lungful's of unpleasant salty water. As I grew more fatigued, the sea began to get the better of me.

When it proved possible to find the strength to surface, I could not clear the water from my lungs in time before the next wave engulfed me. I was drowning.

Panicking, I tried to swim harder, but my legs could kick no longer. My limp arms floated up, and I found myself sinking to the bottom.

After a short struggle, too exhausted to continue, I let myself be taken by the sea.

Sinking slowly towards the ocean floor, the last air bubbles left my mouth.

It was all so beautiful, serene and calm, like imagining the entry to some paradise.

Then I heard music like angels singing, sensing the presence of people around me, whispering. There was no panic or pain, just an overwhelming, all-encompassing, boundless warmth and love. To my surprise, I could see and even breathe underwater.

A strange light engulfed me, bright and beautiful.

I could look directly into it without squinting. Then I saw my grandmother's face, and her hand reached out to hold mine.

'Don't be afraid. You are with us now,' she said.

'I'm not dead, Grandma, am I? I don't want to die yet. I mean I … *can't* die yet.'

Then I saw my father and mother. They reached out their arms and embraced me, their love palpable upon looking into their eyes.

'Dad, Mam, I love you, but can't die yet,' I implored them. 'I can't die yet. I have to get back to Isabel and my children. They need me.'

What I also meant but did not say was, *and I need them.*

It was my first thought of them for such a time, for so very long, having wilfully pushed them out of my mind as far as it was possible due to all the pain of their loss.

Their faces seemed to dance before me, saying *please don't leave us again.* The unborn twins, so tiny and fragile, sent love to me, love that slammed into my chest.

With that, a vortex swirled me away, and the beloved faces faded into the distance.

I rose from the depths to meet a large wave, which carried me on its crest until it finally broke, and my limp body floated face down on its wash.

My feet reached down to meet a sandy floor and I stood up, coughing and spluttering for air until all the sea water had been forced from my lungs.

I slowly regained my senses and made my way above the waterline. The beach was deserted, and the sun shone brightly. Backwards, my body fell onto the soft sand, finding itself unconscious before landing.

***

I came round to a faint yapping close to my ear, then felt something licking my chin. Startled, I turned my head quickly and saw an animal frantically wagging its tail. It looked very similar to a labrador retriever pup with its short, sandy coloured hair and long flappy ears. There was a white patch around its eye which matched one on its stomach. Most strikingly, it had a mane like that of a horse, running from the back of its neck to its tail. Standing on its hind legs, it padded at my face with its front paws.

I sat up and lifted the tiny thing, stroking it with my finger while it whimpered.

By the sounds and the look of it, it had to be only a pup. *Where's your Mama?*

It looked too young to be on its own. I turned it over.

'Oooh, you're a little girl, are you?' I said, stroking her. 'Don't worry, I will mind you. Reckon you and I could really use a friend right now.' I struggled to get to my bare feet with the pup in my arms, and then walked a good distance through uncomfortably hot, dry sand to the top of the highest dune which stretched along the sand bar.

I searched the surroundings for any sign of inhabitants, houses or roads, but there were none. Purple-blossomed mushroom hedgerows and green meadows reached away for miles until they rose up to meet the bright sky.

Walking face-on to the scented breeze, a frisson of wonder passed through me at being alone in this vast landscape. It seemed like a new beginning. I was free.

A blue-spotted six-legged animal with a giraffe-like neck wandered right up to me, looked at me with curiosity, and then went on its way. Multi-coloured fur balls bounced up and down beside my feet, unconcerned by my presence.

In a meadow, a small stream flowed. Kneeling, I cupped the water with my hands, drinking and splashing the refreshing elixir on my face and neck. The pup lapped up water beside me too. *I'd better give you a name*, I thought. *Nobby, that's it*.

I wished the real Nobby could be with me. It seemed a suitable tribute to call the dog after my best pal, the one who had been at my side, more or less, for so long.

From a pouch in my leggings, I took out a sachet, bit it open and squeezed some food out onto my finger. The pup greedily licked it off. I squeezed out more and more until she had eaten her fill. Refreshed, we continued exploring inland.

After a while, I needed to rest, so lay down on the ground and stretched out on an unexpectedly convenient bed of springy moss, a comfortable natural mattress.

Lying there with my eyes half closed against the sun's glare, I could sense the clouds meandering across the now familiar rainbow-laden blue sky.

The sun had been high when I had fallen asleep, and it must have been the next morning when I awoke to the sound of Nobby yapping and darting around. I went to sit up and bizarrely couldn't, apparently somehow pinned to the ground.

Frozen with fear, my first thought was that the Greys had found me again. I turned my head and from the corner of my eye, saw fifty or so strange creatures.

But these were not Greys—far from it.

They also looked like leprechauns, but smaller. What they lacked in size, however, they more than made up for in ferocity. Their spears were raised menacingly above their heads, undoubtedly poised and ready to launch at me.

There was no confusing their meaning, their intent. I was not supposed to be here. But hell, I had just escaped death.

'You're some ugly bastards!' I roared at them, making them jump back.

Trying to get loose, jerking and twisting, I pulled hard at the line holding down my right arm. It sliced painfully into my skin, but I began to work free of it, then turned my head to the opposite side to see at least fifty more of these creatures, assembled in a military formation in front of me.

'Reidh, aidhm, tine!' the call came from the formation.

With that, an archer let fly with his bow.

Through the air flew an arrow the size of a long kebab stick. It pierced deep into my right shoulder and hurt like a very nasty sting. The pain helped me decide to stop struggling, not knowing what other weapons they might have to unleash on me.

When I offered no further resistance, another call came, 'Bia agus Uisce!' and with that, the little beings walked up to me, holding bite-sized bread loaves above my mouth. I lay on my back, nodded and opened my mouth to signal acceptance.

They dropped the bread in, followed by an assortment of sweet fruit.

When I'd had my fill, I shook my head left to right.

They then lifted what to them was a bucket but to me, only a cup. It was full of water which they slowly tipped between my parted lips.

My eyes darted from side to side, watching them intently, considering their size. If I freed myself, I could kick them into the air one at a time, and stamp down on the others. Since they had fed me, however, I felt bound by the laws of hospitality to show gratitude for such an enjoyable meal. Besides, I was feeling curiously mellow by now.

I found out later that the arrow in my shoulder had been tipped with a tranquiliser. I had no place to go, and my stomach was full, so I accepted my fate and soon fell fast asleep, my dog-creature lying beside me.

Later, I awoke on a trolley upon which they had transported me to what looked like an outdoor prison. Nobby was lying on my stomach, so I wrapped her gently in my hands as I sat up to discover an iron clamp bound one of my ankles. From it hung a chain, anchored to the ground about ten metres outside the cage in which I now found myself. Its door was large enough to allow me to crawl in and out.

The cage was about twice my length and wide enough for about six people of my size to lie down. The solid, flat roof allowed me to stand comfortably. Three walls were made of stone, the door and front wall of metal bar.

I crawled out through the doorway, getting to my feet.

Some distance beyond the length of the chain, a row of tiny, elegantly dressed individuals. who I assumed to be nobility, sat in chairs.

In the middle of the row, two even more resplendent creatures, possibly a king and queen, were seated on ornate thrones. Behind them knelt a row of archers, and behind them stood soldiers with spears.

They surveyed me with great curiosity, pointing and turning to chat to one another.

The king then stood up from his chair and approached me.

He stood erect, and all his motions were graceful and majestic. His dress was bright and extravagant; jewels adorned his gold crown, and from beneath it, his long greying hair was blown by the breeze. He gripped his sword, drawn and presumably ready to defend himself should I break loose. He was knee height, his sword six inches long; the hilt and scabbard were gold and encrusted with diamonds.

When he spoke, his voice was clear and surprisingly loud, but I still knelt to listen.

After all, I did assume him to be a king.

'Can you understand what I am saying?'

He indicated to me to nod if I did, so I nodded. Besides, I had the translator device in my ear, enabling me to follow what they were saying.

'I am King Cnogba,' he announced regally. 'You have trespassed into the land of Gan Fheoil and should understand that you have been captured by *Na Fianna,* my elite guards, and you should be grateful I have spared your life. You will remain chained to the ground until such time as I have decided what to do with you. I hereby name you *Sliabh Ard,* which translates as tall mountain, as you are the size of a mighty rock.'

He then retreated to his entourage, and while the nobility looked on, cooks and servants brought out food and drink on tables. The soldiers then broke formation and carried the tables to within the length of my chain.

After the meal, consisting mainly of fruit, I felt extremely pressed by the call of nature, which was no wonder as almost two days had passed since I'd last had the opportunity to relieve myself. But as the king, royalty and guards were watching, I attempted to creep behind my cage to show some attempt at discretion.

To my frustration and with growing desperation, the length of the chain only allowed me to enter my cage, leaving me with no choice but to discharge my body of its burgeoning load onto the trolley that had transported me.

I then shifted it back outside.

This amused the men, but the ladies had seen enough, choosing to retire for the evening. The queen was revolted at what she had witnessed and suggested that I be relocated to the far side of the kingdom.

I sat cross-legged on the ground.

A tall, skinny, stooped leprechaun with a pointed nose stepped forward.

Flanked by guards though still beyond the reach of my chain, he spoke using a megaphone to read these charges against me.

'I, Lord Polpus, Attorney General to the Crown, am instructed by His Majesty to inform you of the following: You are accused of being a trespasser, assumed to be a carnivore and have entered the Kingdom of Gan Fheoil without the express permission of his Majesty King Cnogba. If found guilty, you will be poisoned, and your flesh will be burned away with acid, leaving only your scoured bones.

'From your bones, we shall build a monument to stand at our shore as a warning to any other trespassing carnivores not to enter His Majesty's kingdom. Your trial will take place after you are taught how to speak in our tongue. To this end, a tutor will be assigned to you.' With that, he left.

I retired to my cage with a heavy heart, sitting down on the floor and shaking with fear. I was guilty as accused, and the thoughts of the punishment terrified me.

All the earlier enthusiasm I had felt now left me, leaving me lying in the cage thinking about Cahir, Lal and their dad.

I missed them and longed for the kindness and comfort they had shown me. As for my family back on Earth, I had resigned myself to the belief that they were gone forever and that it would be far better for them to assume I was dead.

***

In the morning, through the bars of my cage, I could see more food had been laid out on the table outside, crawling over to investigate. It looked like porridge with milk and a selection of unfamiliar fruit. I was fully sated by the time I had eaten my way through it, slowly ambling back to my cage to lie down.

As I did so, three puppet-sized females walked towards my door.

A prominent girl, much taller than the other two, walked gracefully. She was slim with a pear-shaped figure and long golden hair, making her appear to be a cosmopolitan model. She wore a green and gold saree styled dress that reached her ankles. On her feet, she wore jewelled slippers.

She entered my cage with a big smile. 'I am Arielle,' she simply stated.

I scanned her top to toe. There were bracelets on her wrists, and she also wore anklets, rings and dangling earrings. A lovely perfume wafted about her.

In my lying position, I supported my head with my hand under my chin so that our eyes were then at the same level. My free hand reached out to shake hers but realising how huge my hand was in proportion to hers, I offered just my index finger instead.

Smiling, she shook it.

She was polite and friendly, so when she requested that I lay on my back so her assistants could fasten a collar around my neck, I obliged. Afterwards, she pointed to her dress. 'You see this dress?' she asked. 'I want you to say what colour it is.'

A strange question. Any fool could have seen that it was yellow! What was she up to? Did she think she was speaking to some kind of idiot?

'It's yellow,' I voiced.

Yet a wholly different word came out of my mouth—'*bui*'. This continued as we spoke. Whenever I thought I was saying a word or phrase in English, this other tongue was freed into the air, my own words disappearing as if dissipating on a breeze.

Somehow, these words were being translated into Diazian, akin to a form of Gaelic. Up until then, I had only been able to understand what was being said, but now, with the collar attached to my neck, I could speak it too, and effortlessly.

Arielle explained that she was responsible for my welfare and for teaching me Diazian laws and customs so I could comprehend the arguments at my trial. She believed it was wrong to keep me tethered to the ground, offering to do all she could to make me as comfortable as possible. I was in a wildlife park, she explained, a place which held many species but none that in any way could match me for size.

Here lived many unusual forms of animals, including herds of creatures that looked like elephants; the largest about three feet tall with huge tusks.

Every time they passed, they stopped and roared. I was the only restrained animal, however; the others were free to roam, and all seemed well-fed and happy.

In time, I got to know the staff who prepared my food and laid out the table for me.

'You're going to cause a famine with the amount of food you eat!' they joked.

The mathematicians had calculated from my height and girth that I should be fed 148 times the amount of food they themselves might eat.

So, they fed me what must have appeared to them as gargantuan meals three times a day, eating at a table and chair proportioned to my height. I had clean, running water to wash with and a to-scale toilet which had been designed and built especially for me.

Three meals a day! That's just like home, I thought, *even if it is vegetables.*

Later, however, when lunch was laid out, I was pleasantly surprised to see a plate of what looked and tasted like cocktail sausages with bread, which I duly demolished and would gladly have eaten more.

That evening, there were what seemed liked meat patties for dinner with a wide selection of unrecognisable vegetables. There was plenty to eat in just that one sitting, leaving me feeling overstuffed after clearing the lot. I had thought the Gan Fheoil were vegetarians, but those had been very tasty meaty meals, among the best I'd ever had.

I then went off to bed, but couldn't sleep, my mind always preoccupied by thoughts of my future.

I was going to be chained to the ground until the day of my trial, found guilty, mortally poisoned and my body scorched with acid.

All sorts of disturbing thoughts raced through my head.

There were thoughts of Isabel, too, left alone. Would she ever remarry? If she did, then hopefully, it would not be too soon for although I wanted her to be happy, it was torture to consider another man in our bed. A man who would also assume the role as the father of my children, including my unborn twins. The love I had shared and the life I had built with Isabel, the fun I'd had with my children, watching their activities in the playgrounds and the park as they were growing up … All that was now gone.

I fell into a deep depression.

***

The next morning, as I was sitting on the ground finishing a breakfast of fruit and a selection of bread and jams, the three ladies approached once more.

'Am I disturbing your breakfast?' Arielle asked. 'I was hoping we could start your tutoring today if you are feeling up to it. I also wanted to talk to you about your welfare. Are you warm at night? Are you happy with your meals? If there is anything I can do to make your stay pleasanter, please let me know.'

I told her I wasn't feeling up to any lessons and returned to inside my cage. I was convinced I would never be happy again, so why bother? There was no reason to talk to her, merely wanting to be left alone. After all, they would soon put me to death, and anyway, with nobody around who I loved or who loved me, what was the point?

I decided I was going to eat myself to death.

The next time Arielle visited, I told her I wanted twice as much food, and the next day, I duly received as much as I could eat. After that, each time she tried to approach me, I ignored her. It was very hard not to be nice back to somebody who as constantly being nice to me, but I managed it, and still, I would gorge myself on more and more food, growing fatter and fatter.

As my waistline extended, so too did my hideous black state of morose solitude and depression, something that never left me from dawn till it was time to sleep each day.

Every night, upon falling asleep, terrifying memories from my abduction would creep into my mind. One night, they appeared with such intensity that I lost control of my mind. My breath came in gasps; it felt terrible, like the end.

I'm going to black out. What if this is really it?

My heart was hammering inside my chest as if trying to escape from me. The cage spun, leaving me feeling horribly sick as I lay on the floor trying to make everything slow down to something my brain and body could cope with.

I wanted to call to somebody, but there was no one. I was alone in blackness... creeping blackness. So, I lay on the floor in the foetal position.

Where am I? What's my name? Who can I call out to?

Then I heard a familiar calling. *'Paddy, Paddy, Paddy!'*

I looked up and there, hovering in front of me, was the apparition of Muhammad Ali once more. Rays of light were radiating from his body, and the darkness went away.

His bare, black chest glistened as he stood there in his white boxing shorts and gloves, his black wings fully unfurled behind his back.

'Peace be with you, Paddy,' he said. *'Worrying about what might happen just wastes precious time. You have been appointed to save humanity. Remember this:*

'Even the Greatest were once beginners. Don't be afraid to take the first step. Make a point of doing something great every day! Don't count the days; make the days count!'

The panting began to subside, and the terror left me.

'Thanks for the advice,' I muttered. 'But hey, didn't you see the fiasco of that riot you suggested I initiated on the spaceship? Now I'm chained to the ground in the middle of nowhere, so how can you possibly suggest I *make the days count?*'

Ali ruffled his magnificent wings. *'What you're thinking is what you're becoming,'* he said and flew off. With that, the light faded until all was pitch dark again.

It was always darkest just before the dawn, leaving me watching intently as the sun peeped up from the horizon, my heart racing with enthusiasm at the brand-new day.

Make a point of doing something great every day; make the days count.

It sounded inspiring, but what did Ali have in mind?

I looked down to see my obese belly—maybe getting rid of that would be a good start—and then I should get fit again, too. That morning, after a standard-sized bowl of porridge and some fruit, training began with great gusto.

It wasn't easy with my foot chained, but I managed to do stretching exercises, push-ups and sit-ups, also walking briskly back and forth as far as the chain allowed.

The catering staff noticed my unusual behaviour and when they looked up at me, I astonished them with a hearty 'Good Morning!' and a big smile.

When Arielle came later that morning, I said, 'Top of the morning to you!' and enthusiastically suggested it was time to start my lessons.

'Goodness be upon you,' she replied. 'I am so excited to have the opportunity to teach you and get to know you.'

Arielle suggested that I lifted her up to stand on the table and lessons began. The first conversation I had with her was about the food, which totally confused me.

'How come I can be put to death for eating meat, but they still bring me sausages, meats, and other tasty, carnivorous meals?

She smiled. 'Ah. That is *replicated* meat, faux meat. I've never tasted real meat, but I'm told it is nearly indistinguishable. Animals are not involved in its production.'

'How come the Gan Fheoil are smaller than the Do Rogha?' I enquired.

'It's because of what they feed the animals. The nuts the livestock consume contain growth enhancers to bulk them up. Then, when the Do Rogha eat the animals, they ingest traces of the enhancers, which make them grow taller, broader and heavier with every generation. The bigger they get, the more meat they need to sustain themselves.

'The Greys that abducted you are not from this planet,' she explained. 'They are the workforce of the Do Rogha fishing fleet, employed to do the manual work they won't do themselves. The spacecraft are operated remotely by Do Rogha pilots.

'We Gan Fheoils have our own fleet of spacecraft, and though we strongly disagree with the maltreatment of animals, there is nothing we can do to stop it. We had been at war with the Do Rogha for a long time, and a fragile truce exists between us. To try and stop their slave trade would constitute a declaration of war.'

Another question I had was how come I had disembarked from a vessel so technically advanced, to a land of inhabitants armed with swords, spears, bows and arrows?

Technology had become too advanced for the good of the inhabitants of Diaz, Arielle said. Artificial

Intelligence had grown to a point where people felt useless, and social media had become so essential that citizens could not interact without using it.

Citizens preferred to stay at home, interacting by social media, getting everything delivered to their homes by drones.

Adults had grown fat and lazy, and all the children had become unhappy.

'Ultimately, it was better to limit the availability of technology and return to depending on our own abilities. After all,' she said, 'meeting other beings is the most important part of life. A new slogan was born: *I'd rather real people to computers.*

Arielle went on to tell me she had lost her partner, a Gan Fheoil trooper, who had gone missing after a territorial clash with the Do Rogha while on a border patrol. They had never cloned children, and she had never married again.

I bowed my head to indicate sorrow for her.

In time, Arielle and I became good friends. As well as her beauty, there was sweetness in the tone of her voice, and she would use her charm to make herself agreeable to everyone she met. Because of her, I was more tolerant of my captivity.

'Don't dwell on your past,' she would say. 'That's gone, and for all you know, it might have been a dream. As for the future, nobody knows what that will bring, so there is no point worrying about that either. You are a child of the universe, no less than the stars, your life unfolding as it was intended to. With all the awful things that have happened to you, it is still a beautiful universe. Be cheerful and try to be happy.'

I thought about Ali's advice, *Make a point of doing something great every day*.

In my situation, all I could do was to try and be friendly.

From then on, I greeted everybody with kindness.

For safety, visitors to the park were forbidden to come within reach of my chain in fear that I might injure them, accidentally or otherwise, but I always waved and tried to amuse them as they passed. It was reported at the very highest levels that I was a friendly and benign individual. More and more visitors came to the park.

When asked what they enjoyed most about their visit, the answer was generally me, *the Giant*. They also complained about how saddened they felt to see me restrained while the rest of the wildlife were free to roam.

Arielle encouraged my new, healthy lifestyle.

She had fashionable stretchy polka-dot outfits and shoes in bright colours made for me, taking time to notice when I had changed them and letting me know how they looked on me. She organised stylists to tend to my hair and was critical of their work.

She organised the cooks to prepare special meals and a crew to wash me each evening after I finished eating. I felt pleasurably pampered.

Her feelings for me became obvious to all who worked at the park. She even wrote a petition to the king requesting that, while awaiting trial, I should be freed from my chain, explaining that in her professional opinion, I posed no threat to the visitors, staff, or the other wildlife.

It was countersigned by the curator and all the park wardens.

The petition was received by His Majesty, and by return, Arielle received a letter outlining the terms of my release which she read out to me.

- *Sliabh Ard must not leave the wildlife park without the permission of His Majesty*
- *Sliabh Ard must remain a dutiful and loyal subject to His Majesty*
- *Sliabh Ard is to take good care not to trip over or*

otherwise harm His Majesty's subjects or animals and is not to pick anyone up without their consent.

*In return for the above, Sliabh Ard is to be **released from the chain**.*

With great cheerfulness, I stood with my hand on my heart, agreed to the terms, and swore to be His Majesty's loyal subject.

Chapter 12: Rise to Fame

Free of my chain, I could now do a lot more than merely wave to amuse the visitors. I did handstands and stood on my head, which everyone loved to watch. People came to the park just to see me perform. Forward rolls joined my repertoire too, equally popular.

One beautiful, bright day, I was full of the joys of life, and when I saw Arielle, I began to sing her an Irish song.

Of all the stars that ever shone
Not one does twinkle like your pale blue eyes;
Like golden corn at harvest time, your hair ...
Walking by the beach, the wind
Gently blows and fills your hair;
Your sweet-scented breath is everywhere.

No matter where I wander, I'm still haunted
by your name
The portrait of your beauty stays the same.
Standing by my cage, wondering where you are,
when you'll return again,
That is the love I have for Arielle.

All who heard it stopped to listen and after the song finished, complete silence followed. Then one person clapped, and more joined in until they were all hollering and cheering.

It was agreed by all that it was the most romantic song they had ever heard.

From that day on, visitors flocked to the park. Arielle would introduce me, and I would sing and dance and do acrobatics for them. The astonished audience loved it.

They sang along to any tune, and my songs quickly became popular, the Gan Fheoilians copying me as I sang quickly, becoming a fashionable pastime that allowed people to have fun. There was constant demand for more material. I tried to remember the tunes I knew, and if I did not know the words, just made some up.

After my shows, the Gan Fheoil held parties in small private rooms with friends and took turns at singing. The art of singing and dancing had all but been forgotten in Gan Fheoil. It became apparent that I was initiating a cultural shift.

Soon, microphones were placed in common areas at social events, and the inhabitants would anxiously wait their turn to perform.

The new singing phenomenon was considered the ultimate in fun. These normally introverted beings began to perform in front of audiences that included strangers. From what I heard, they sang loudly and badly, but their audience always enjoyed it.

The wildlife park was constantly full and would have been if it were twice the size.

Realising the demand, Arielle asked if I would like to turn our routine into a full show in the municipal stadium, where folks must pay to see the entertainment.

I agreed, under the condition that we would be a double act.

She loved the idea. Bursting with excitement, she wanted to hear my suggestions and was keen that we get started immediately. Since nobody had seen the likes of me before, we agreed to name the show 'Sliabh Ard: the Giant Who Fell to Diaz'.

We performed in an open circular theatre, the central stage surrounded by tiers of seats arranged in a steep slope to give two hundred thousand spectators a perfect view.

I was to make my entrance along a tunnel at the same level as the stage.

It was barely wide enough for me to crawl through.

Arielle, who straddled my neck, had to lie flat to avoid the ceiling.

We waited there behind red curtains till we heard the ringmaster announce, *'A dhaoine uasile, failte roimh an seo is mo leis an realta is mo sa chruinne, Sliabh Ard!'*

It translated as, 'Ladies and Gentlemen, welcome to the greatest show with the largest star in the universe, Sliabh Ard!'

The announcement was followed by a fanfare of trumpets.

The show began after dusk. Torches surrounded the stage, and a spotlight tower was directed at the red curtains. Flames shot into the air, the audience cheering and applauding as the curtain opened and I appeared.

I crawled to the centre of the stage, where I reared up on my knees, letting out a ferocious roar and causing the audience to jump back in their seats.

Arielle held on with her legs either side of my neck, ropes attached around my head.

I then returned to all fours, holding my left arm and right leg out straight for a count of ten, followed by my right arm and left leg.

The crowd cheered and waved flags, which were green with gold trim and had *Sliabh Ard* printed on them.

Then, to allow Arielle to dismount, I dropped my shoulders close to the ground, leaving my backside in the air.

After the fanfare of trumpets had stopped, she cracked her bullwhip three times against the ground to announce the beginning of the performance.

First, I warmed up, stretching, swinging my arms and kicking my legs high into the air. Then, standing on one leg, I performed a series of front thigh-stretching exercises, leaning forward into a crane-like stance. This invariably elicited polite applause from the crowd, impressed that such a mighty creature could hold such a position.

Arielle cracked her whip again, and despite the limited space available, I did a few forward rolls which the audience found exciting because of the delicious chance I might not measure one correctly and end up flattening some of the ringside spectators.

I then stood on my head, and the crowd held their breath in case I fell over and my huge feet landed on top of members the audience.

She cracked her whip again, and I crawled back out through the tunnel, put on my hard-toed dancing shoes and a kilt, and reappeared to do a hard tap Irish dance routine which, as children, we had all been taught in school in Dublin.

The audience marvelled at the dexterity and fleetness of foot of such a colossus and joined in, imitating the dancing, singing along to the choruses of the Irish songs.

The show was hailed by the critics as a sensation, the likes of which had never been seen before. Every Gan Fheoilian wanted to see it first-hand. What had started out as pranks in the wildlife park had become the most popular act in the kingdom and was still showing no sign of losing its appeal.

I was famous, and now intended to use this new-found fame to my advantage.

At the end of each show, after saluting the audience, I bellowed out, *'Ta me ag iarraidh a dhul abhaile,'* or 'I want to go home'.

Arielle joined me. *'Lig do dul abhaile,'* she sang, which meant *let him go home.*

She then started a chant of *'Saoirse, Saoirse, Saoirse—freedom, freedom, freedom*—with which the crowd joined in, the children being particularly supportive of me.

They drew pictures of me in school and made banners, pleading on my behalf that I be allowed to go home. King

Cnogba also came to see the show and enjoyed it so much that he visited me personally the next day.

I told him my story from the time of my abduction, pleading with him to be pardoned and returned to Earth. With my ever-increasing popularity, what would the Gan Fheoilian population say, anyway, if I were found guilty?

I had used my time wisely. Such was the enthusiasm for my release that the press was suggesting all charges against me be dropped.

Lord Polpus was horrified at the suggestion that there should be no trial.

He had dedicated his life to studying how to make lies out of the truth and truth out of lies, and he knew how to draw and squeeze every drop out of the seemingly most inconsequential of details. He lobbied King Cnogba's politicians.

Even the greatest of kings would view the world through the eyes of their advisors, so when they counselled him that the trial should be heard, King Cnogba agreed.

There were two charges, the first being that of trespassing since Gan Fheoilian law strictly prohibited anyone to enter its land without a visa.

The second charge was that of being a carnivore as whole generations of Gan Fheoilian citizens had given their lives in the defence of animals. On any visa application, you had to state that you did not eat meat and had never done so.

Every time my hearing was due, it was postponed by the prosecution, who maintained there was a lack of disclosure on my part and they needed more time to build their case. Throughout these protracted machinations, the show continued and each night, after the performance, I drank a barrel of their wine, about a litre.

To celebrate the thousandth performance, a party was held after the curtain closed.

Everybody seemed to be having a wonderful time while I sat alone, watching them. Even sitting on the ground, I was far above the crowd, unable to hear anybody's words. So, the show's star, who should have been the centre of attention, felt excluded.

It was late, and I was worn out from the long run of performances. I got down on all fours and crawled into my cage where I lay on my side, trying to get comfortable.

Arielle soon followed me in. 'I saw you leaving. Was I neglecting you?'

She raised her tiny arms, showing the palms of her hands as if to say, *Here I am*.

'You have become so important to me, Paddy. In you, my life becomes whole, and with you, my days grow bright. In your arms I would love to lie, this night and for the rest of my life.' She meekly looked down at her feet. 'I want to be with you forever.' She raised her eyes to mine. 'We are meant to be together. Will you marry me?'

I shook my head in disbelief. 'Are you crazy, Arielle? For a start, I'm about ten times bigger than you are. How could we ever have a family together?'

'No! No!' she said. 'You don't understand. This planet has different customs to yours. On Diaz, inhabitants do not get married only to start families.

'Males marry males, females marry females. The only thing that matters is that they are in love. And I love you.'

I reddened. 'Sure. Well, we do that on earth too,' I told her. 'But interspecies marriage is a bit … unorthodox.'

'It hasn't happened on Diaz yet, either. But if you love me, we could be the first. You *do* love me, Paddy, don't you?'

'I do! And I'd love to marry you, but unfortunately, I'm already married, and my current wife would *not* let me. Most people on Earth don't even believe in life on other planets. What if I returned to tell my whole world that there is indeed life, and I have gone and married an extra-terrestrial? What would Isabel—my wife—say?'

I felt relieved and better about myself with this measured answer.

She talked about the great times we'd had together and the strong bond that we had forged. Furthermore, I was forced to remember that Isabel was light years away.

And the biggest point she made was that Isabel would never, ever know.

We discussed our relationship until I heard the night rain falling. It was cold.

Arielle shivered and moved to snuggle into me.

Lying on my side, I reached for a blanket to cover us. Careful not to crush her against my arm, I fell asleep.

***

Next morning, we were both happily snoozing together when we were awoken by the sound of scuffling outside.

Suddenly, a troop of photographers and journalists burst into my cage. It soon became apparent that we had been spied on during the night, judging by the personal questions they were asking Arielle about our relationship … and whether we had become more than friends.

Arielle refused to either confirm or deny their accusations, telling them it was not their business what we did at night and that we intended to be married.

They tried to question me too, but I told them to get out of my sight as I was about to get very annoyed. I followed this with a threat to pick them up and drop them in my dung pile. At this, they left quickly. The news of our intended marriage quickly made the headlines on all media platforms, accompanied, of course, by the many photos of us sleeping together.

Chapter 13: The Trial

When my case eventually went to trial, it took place at the wildlife park where a courtroom had been custom built for the event. The judge was a lady who wore a rainbow-coloured sequin bodysuit with a headdress of feathers to match. She sat behind a desk elevated above the solicitors, barristers and other officers of the law.

They wore pink, square-cut coats, richly laced with gold and round, pale blue hats. Below them sat the jury, looking up at the proceedings.

I sat well-groomed, wearing a green jumpsuit in the same chair beside the table I used for everyday dining. My seat was at the same level but a distance from the judge.

She instructed me to remain seated during the proceedings.

To either side of the legal teams was a gallery which seated Arielle and invited citizens of high esteem.

The *Iris na Seirbhise Cuirteanna,* the court service, had never presented a trial quite like this one. It had first captivated Gan Fheoil and then, through news broadcasts, had spread to include the whole of the planet.

Opening Speech for the Prosecution, Presented by Lord Polpus.

'May it please the Breitheamh—the judge—and persons of the jury. Sliabh Ard was arrested soon after arriving at the shores of Gan Fheoil, being here in person and without a visa. Generations of Gan Fheoil have shed blood and given their lives in the defence of our borders. The defendant was sedated, and while he slept, we ascertained from his size, bulk and teeth that he was a carnivore, a killer and devourer of animals.

'As such, he also has no right to be in our lands. In fact, our mathematicians calculate that he is responsible for the deaths of an *inordinate number* of animals.

'Moreover, since his capture, he has brought the singing and dancing craze which has led to riotous, drunken parties, where our young citizens seem to feel such wanton, untethered elation that they think there is no tomorrow.

'Furthermore, any morals they may previously have held are casually abandoned.

'I have written many articles with the determination to try to uphold the morals of Gan Fheoil. With regard to any article I have written in which I have shared my low opinion of Sliabh Ard and Arielle, I withdraw nothing. I ask you, is it appropriate that the inhabitants of Gan Fheoil should open their morning papers to see a woman sleeping with an alien beast ten times her size? There is something wholly unnatural about it.

'I would also like to introduce into this case, files lodged at the Diazian planning authorities, in which the Greys, having observed at a distance the low life form called *humans,* have made their case that they were fit for general consumption.

'This is based upon the complete lack of respect and the cruelty inflicted by these humans on the animals in their care. I have here today the report filed with the authorities from which you may draw your conclusion and consider a just judgement.'

He presented shocking statistics about the treatment of animals on Earth, showing the jury video footage of the cruelty of factory farming.

He explained how human activity had caused famine, spread disease, and was the cause of pollution, smog and stock depletion. Due to humans' complete disrespect for animals, many species on the planet had become extinct.

'They have cleared fifty percent of the world's rainforests,' Polpus continued. 'They have destroyed fifty percent of their coral reefs, poisoning their rivers and whole swathes of the ocean with plastics. Their emissions have covered their atmosphere with a smog that has led to increasing global temperatures, all of which has now created a very real existential threat to their civilisation.

'The greatest crime of all, however, is that they know what they are doing. You would have thought they might have changed their ways when informed of the impending catastrophe, but they have not, preferring to leave the problem to their next generations. Whoever understands the nature of humans will believe it possible for such a vile animal to be capable of every action I have claimed. And consider this: if their intellect and cunning were to evolve, then what would happen if they became a force powerful enough to begin to travel through the universe?'

Polpus went on to suggest that all humans should be exterminated, or if not, at the very least the males should be castrated so that, in time, the race would die out.

This suggestion was dismissed by the judge, who argued that nature would determine who would survive. The humans may have thought they had developed to be masters of nature, but they would have to learn that they had not become this.

Human behaviour may lead to their own extinction; however, it was also feasible that some prodigy may be born, or some event may happen to lead to their enlightenment. He reminded Polpus that not so many generations ago, his own ancestors had also eaten any form of meat from anywhere in the galaxy.

When interviewed after the day's events, the meat-eating Do Rogha, watching the trial on screens from over the sea, vowed never to eat human meat again, in case they might become contaminated by ingesting such vile and depraved creatures. Members of the jury were shaken at the extent of the evidence amassed against humans.

I felt so ashamed that when asked to respond, I said meekly, 'I admit I was part of the pollution problem, but I didn't know that factory farmed animals were treated so badly. If I had known, I would have campaigned to stop the practice.

'If you should decide to return me to Earth, I will do my utmost to help those poor defenceless creatures.'

The case was then adjourned for the day.

***

Opening Speech for the Defence, Presented by Vergus O'Rilly, my Attorney.

'May it please you, —judge—and citizens of the jury. You have heard the charges against my client, in which the prosecution claims that he entered the Kingdom of Gan Fheoil without obtaining the necessary visa. He is also accused of being a carnivore, but that charge is based solely on his great size and the shape of his teeth.

'Polpus continues to make false and malicious statements regarding Sliabh Ard. These statements are in the dubious form of media articles, in which Polpus states that, *Since Sliabh Ard's arrival on our shores, the morals of the land have been in decline.*

'He also accuses him of inciting the population into late-night singing and dancing sessions which have been closely associated with drunkenness and disorder.

'It is a matter of serious concern that such libellous statements should in any way relate to a creature who has built a high reputation in this land. Polpus has said that his declaration is true and that it is for the public benefit that these statements were made, but who is he to decide what is moral and what is immoral?

'Sliabh Ard has been taken away from his mate and offspring who reside on another planet in another galaxy, light years away. He was beaten and starved on the transport ships that brought him to the Do Rogha and was then used as a beast of burden. In fear of his life, he swam the deepest, widest ocean. Does that not show the purity of his heart?

'He did not want to leave his home and travel to Gan Fheoil; he was taken from his home, and Gan Fheoil landed on him. Without trial, he was bound and dragged to our capital and staked to the ground. While Sliabh Ard was tethered, Polpus read out charges accusing him of being a carnivore and continues to slander him. Now, *that* is immoral.

'He is a victim of the intergalactic animal slave trade, a practice against which generations of Gan Fheoil have shed blood and given their lives to fight.

'He should not have been tethered to the ground. He should have been treated with compassion as a refuge seeker whose arrival on our shores was not of his own making.'

I stood while Vergus questioned me about animals, explaining that not all humans were as depicted at this trial. I went on to say that there were organisations such as the World Wildlife Fund whose mission was specifically to conserve nature and reduce the threats to the diversity of life on Earth. Their vision was to build a future in which people lived in harmony with nature, in fact, seeking save the planet by reconciling the needs of human beings and the needs of other species with which they shared the Earth.

They took up the role of being the voice for those creatures who had no voice.

I declared my love for all animals but especially dogs, going on to say that I had been keeping them since I was a little boy, taking in strays whenever I came across one.

If ever I met an animal in distress, I went to its aid. 'I would never knowingly do harm to any animal,' I stated loudly and then sat back down.

Members of the jury smiled and nodded.

I believed I had done well.

The court broke for a long lunch.

That afternoon, I stood while Polpus cross-examined me.

'What is your perception of the moral condition of Earth?' he opened.

I replied, 'I was never in a position to judge what was moral or immoral but merely to live in the society mapped out for me. Earth's animals and mankind had evolved from eating one another, and to deny that is to deny man's very-existence.

'On Earth, there are many views. The evidence you presented yesterday may be true for a proportion of the population, but the public are unaware of these details. They buy meat wrapped; it comes to them clean and neatly packaged, showing no sign of any animal suffering. Your so-called evidence on the morality of humans did not show that some humans, many of us, want no part in animal suffering. Like the Gan Fheoil, they have elected to become vegetarians and vegans who do not eat meat at all.

'There are also religions which forbid it. Many followers of Hinduism, with one billion devotees, believe the cow is sacred, its milk the only protein they consume.'

'That is all very well but do *you* eat the flesh of animals?' Polpus asked accusingly.

'Yes,' I replied. Unrest and mumbling could be heard from the galleries. 'But only those reared outdoors. It is inevitable that a creature will die. Nothing and no-one can prevent that. The only thing that we can control is how a creature lives, the quality of its life while it is on Earth. I do not eat factory-farmed animals, only animals that have lived a natural life, animals that you see grazing in fields, skipping in meadows. Happy ones.'

'Would you eat a dog, then?' he asked.

'Absolutely not. A dog is a man's best friend. Would *you* eat the flesh of a dog?' I asked, turning the question on him.

'Don't be ridiculous!' Polpus replied with great indignation. 'I would not eat any animal. The very thought of it is disgusting!'

'I beg to differ. You would eat animals. And what's more, you do!' I accused him.

Again, mumbling and unrest could be heard from the gallery.

'All animals eat other animals,' I continued. 'The cattle, sheep and horses that graze happily in the fields—we may think of them as vegetarians but as they chew the grass, they eat billions of microscopic animal organisms. The monkeys in the jungle, when they have eaten enough bananas, hunt for meat. Gigantic whales in the oceans live on animal plankton. Microscopic animals live on the fruit which you eat.

'The only difference between my meat and your meat is that you can't see yours. Are we arguing about whether to eat meat is a crime, or is it the size of the animal you eat that makes you a criminal?'

***

My trial continued for three long days. On the third day, the Breitheamh directed the jury to vote with their conscience. She added that it was, however, her belief that no crime had been committed in the Kingdom of Gan Fheoil.

After hours of deliberation, they found me not guilty.

The judge ruled that I was to be freed and returned to Earth.

'Never ever be afraid to do the right thing, especially if the well-being of a person or other animal is at stake.' The greatness of a civilization can be judged by how they treat their animals,' she stated with supreme conviction.

Finally, she instructed me to keep my word and on my return to Earth, I should urge the population there to bring an end to further animal cruelty of any kind.

'Judge,' I pleaded. 'I am just a nobody on Earth, just one of eight billion people on a planet with a rapidly growing population. What makes you think I can make a difference?'

'Your deepest fear is not what you are unable to do. It is your ability which most frightens you. It is your duty to lead. As you let yourself shine, you unconsciously free others to do the same.

'Now, go and start the Earth's Third World War. In the first two, millions died, and in the third, billions of humans can be saved alongside the whole ecology of your planet. Every human must play their part in this essential war.'

Chapter 14: Leaving Arielle

The bay where Arielle liked to go to was called Gurteen; she had first visited the bay on her honeymoon, and it held treasured memories for her.

Once I had been granted my complete freedom, she insisted that we should go. She'd had a basket made for my back for her to travel in, Nobby following at my heels.

We made our way through the countryside, eventually arriving on a rocky shore to look out at the calm, green ocean.

Arielle had never been fully satisfied that her crew could wash me well enough with clothes and buckets, she said, and today she had brought giant soap bars to facilitate me to bathe properly. She then turned her back to me.

'Go!' she mandated, excitement in her eyes. 'Take off your clothes and go swim!'

It was a bright, very cold day and I didn't fancy swimming. As far as I was concerned, I was clean enough, but Arielle would be disappointed if I didn't bathe.

So I took off my polka dot onesie and waded in.

Once I'd established the cold sea was deep enough, I dived in.

She made her way to a high ledge, shouting instructions from there about how I should bathe properly. Hygiene and cleanliness were crucially important to her.

By the time she was satisfied, I was freezing cold, my teeth chattering as I waded back to the water's edge.

She turned her back again as I was getting out, advocating for my modesty.

Fresh clothes had been laid on a rock with a parcel on top of them.

'They're gifts for you!' she shouted with her back still turned to me.

'I'm dressed! You can turn around now,' I shouted back.

Arielle came down from the high ledge of the rock.

I opened the parcel and took out a pair of royal maroon silk boxer shorts. *What was she thinking when she decided to get them made for me?* I wondered. *But it's the thought that counts!* I thanked her, putting a kiss on my finger and transferring it to her cheek. When I was dressed, she handed me a small box containing a gold ring.

She looked out to sea as she spoke. 'I know you must return to your family on Earth, but remember this: with my soul, my blood, and my bones, I love you. Your face will always be in my mind. Soon, I will never see you again. I'll be so alone without you.'

Her voice broke, weeping.

I was so sorry, too, to be abandoning her.

She opened her arms wide, as if about to burst, asking again, 'Will you marry me?'

Aaaah! Jaysus Christ! Would you believe it?

I didn't want to marry Arielle the idea totally ridiculous to me and me already married but I did recognize our loyalty to and feelings for each other, After all we had been through, I could not bear to see her in distress and feeling abandoned like this. So on the assumption that Isabel would never know and I'd never see Arielle again, I said *yes* to make her happy.

We duly married at a small private ceremony at the park.

Chapter 15: The Journey Home

During the wedding, I could not stop myself from thinking of Isabel and my family, wanting only to get home. The arrangements had been made, and my new wife accompanied me to the space travel portal, showing me how to put on a space onesie.

It lay in a round shape on the ground and all I needed to do was to stand on it to activate it, so it would expand and roll up to my neck.

'Pull it over your head when it's time to jump,' Arielle instructed.

For luck and for Arielle, I pulled my shiny new maroon boxers over the onesie.

The pilot handed me a bag. 'Make sure little Nobby is sitting securely in it when you make the leap,' he said in stern terms, his eyes wide in a silent implication that if I weren't careful, Nobby would tumble out and never be seen again.

Of course, I had insisted Nobby had to come with me.

'Sing it one last time for me,' Arielle asked sadly. I sang the first song which I had intended to sing just for her, but it made us both famous.

I sang it and when the song finished, she could barely look at me.

'You've been the most precious thing in my life, and we were so happy together! Go home. Go home, my love. You don't have a choice. But remember, even if you cannot hear me, I'll be thinking of you always. You have only to look up and know …'

She started to sob again, unable to say more so I dropped down onto all fours. She threw her arms up around my neck, planting a lingering kiss on my cheek.

I boarded a shuttle through the cargo hold entrance. As we waved, knowing it was for the last time, countless tears were shed by both of us.

The shuttle was no bigger than a city car. I held Nobby tight as if my life was depending on it, then assumed a squashed foetal position before the cargo door at the rear could be closed. It was so cramped, *too* cramped and claustrophobic.

How long will this journey be and how will I manage in this level of discomfort?

'Where are we going?' asked the pilot, sitting a level above me in the front.

'Earth,' I said.

'Where to on Earth? It's a big place.'

The first thing that came to my mind was where I had been abducted from.

'Belmullet, County Mayo, Ireland.'

'Sure thing!' said the pilot. 'I think I know where that is but let's just be sure.' How could he know where it was, such a small place? He began to interface with a 3D map of galaxies, closing them from the outside, working his way in until he left only the Milky Way open. He closed down parts of that until all that was left was Earth's solar system. Then, he repeated the process until all that remained was Earth. After that, he enlarged Ireland, zoomed in on Mayo and selected Belmullet. 'That's the one,' he said.

The craft ascended vertically through a rainbow sky into space.

In a short time, he announced that we were orbiting Earth.

I had hoped the shuttle was going to land in Belmullet, but then the pilot called to me from the front. 'Get ready to jump; don't forget the bag!'

Jump to where though? What do you mean?

I put Nobby into the bag and held onto it tightly.

'Ready? May your god go with you! Now go!' said the pilot urgently.

The cargo door opened, and we were sucked out. In a flash, we materialised on a ledge on a cliff face, facing a vast ocean.

Startled, I looked around, assuming it to be Mayo in the west of Ireland but didn't know for sure. Looking out towards the cloudy and dull horizon, I guessed it to be early morning. Then I heard Nobby yap, so let her out of the space bag. She crept to the ledge and started barking down at who knew what.

I stepped closer, seeing how the ledge dropped in a sheer fall to the sea beneath, such a long way down. I backed away from the edge, dizzy at the thought of falling, and trod carefully, looking for a way off the cliff face.

Above, the top of the cliff looked farther away than the sea beneath.

The morning passed, then afternoon and evening. I had spent the day scanning the sea for boats that I might alert to send a rescue party, but none passed. Stuck on a remote hidden ledge on a sheer cliff in County Mayo, I might have to wait a very long time before alerting potential rescuers. Night fell, and sitting with my back pressed against the ledge, I fell asleep under a full moon, Nobby snuggled on my lap.

I awoke at dawn to the sound of *ga, ga, ga* and *gawl-ool-ah.* Seagulls were screaming at each other and perhaps wondering what I was doing in their nests.

I shivered, the distant snow-capped mountains reminded me of how cold it could be here. A pale sun ascended slowly in the sky, its weak heat welcome on my bare head.

The seagulls, masters of the art of flight, skimmed the waves, diving for fish.

We'd had no food or a drink since before boarding the ship and were going to starve to death. The day stretched ahead, a repeat of yesterday.

Exhausted and desperate, my head lolled into my hands.

After travelling through the galaxies, I am going to die alone on an Irish cliff face. The irony of it was not lost on me. It seemed like the ultimate in bad jokes.

Then, I looked up and floating in mid-air in front of me was another apparition of the great Muhammad Ali. The great wind persistently ruffled the feathers of his wings, but he hovered there, perfectly still as if finding himself in a breezeless atmosphere.

He frowned as he looked me in the eye.

'Have you learnt nothing?' he asked. 'Didn't I tell you? Live every day as if it were your last because someday, you're going to be right! You're just going to sit here and starve to death on this cliff face?'

Then, with a swish of his wings, he soared straight up towards the sun until I could see him no longer. I thought for a moment.

It's now or never. I picked up Nobby, held her firmly under my arm and edged slowly out to the brink of the ledge. With a loud scream, I jumped outwards and down into space. Terror seized me, my heart seeming to stop.

I heard the whoosh of wind in my ears but it only lasted moments.

Remembering not to land on my back, I straightened my legs, so they were the first part of me to meet the green sea. Once under water, I let go of Nobby, attempting to swim to the surface. I was tired and weak with hunger, unable to rise fast enough.

In my terror, I had forgotten to take a lungful of air before entering the water, now desperately needing to inhale. I could hold on no longer, opening my mouth, the briny water filling my lungs. I sank further and further, watching the last air bubbles leave me during the long drift towards the ocean floor.

Then, as before, a strange, white light engulfed me. There was a whispering around. Then I saw my grandmother's face again, and her hand reached out to mine.

'Don't be afraid; you are with us now.'

'I'm not dead, Grandma, am I? I can't die now, not after all I've been through. I'm nearly home, and I have so much to do with my life. Muhammad Ali told me I was appointed by God to save mankind and I promised a judge I'd succeed.'

My father and mother appeared beside her.

'Don't be silly! Come with us. It's time, son; you've had enough.'

'But Dad, Mam—I can't die yet. Heaven can wait! I want to get home to Isabel and the children. I haven't even seen our twins yet.'

My mother turned to my father and grandmother.

'Do you know what? He hasn't changed a bit since he was a child. I remember screaming at him from the front garden to come in for his dinner while he was playing football in the street. He stubbornly refused to listen then! It was always, 'Next goal's the winner, Ma!' He's still the same.'

In an instant, a current swept me away.

From the thirteenth tee box at Barna Golf Course, I had once watched in awe as mighty Atlantic waves, as large as houses, rolled and crashed on the seashore, and now, I was at the bottom of one. Looking up, a giant wave was towering over me.

As if on a roller coaster, I spun from the bottom to the top of the wave. And then I was washed up close to the shore, where I could stand.

Nobby was close by in the water, and when I called to her, she paddled furiously towards me. I waded in her direction, grabbing hold of her with much relief.

We then made our way to the rocky beach.

Chapter 16: Western Strands Hotel

Looking around, I recognised some of the houses, the sight of familiar places a great relief. Dripping wet, I walked up from the beach with my maroon boxers over my orange spacesuit, Nobby under my arm. On reaching the main street, the few locals there blinked, shook their heads, and took a second look.

I walked into the bar of the Western Strands Hotel in Belmullet, which fell quiet as staff and customers turned to stare.

'Paddy, look at the get up of you!' said Kenny the barman. 'Have you been to a fancy-dress party? You look like Superman, gone wrong!'

This greatly amused the usual lads who were permanently perched on the same bar stools, drinking pints for a living.

One stared at Nobby, who was still dripping. 'Where d'you get the rat from?'

'Careful,' I warned him. 'Insult me, but don't insult my dog.'

'Is that what it is?'

Kenny asked casually, 'Seriously though, where did you get to, Paddy? People have been looking for you. The phone hasn't stopped.'

I swallowed. This was going to sound stupid. 'I'm just back from outer space.'

The locals at the bar laughed loudly.

I followed up, 'And I'm in bad need of a pint of Guinness. And give me five packets of cheese and onion crisps, the same of peanuts and you'd better make it two pints.'

'Gone on outta dat, Paddy, ya boy, ya,' came a roar from along the counter. They raised their glasses. 'Back from outer space no less—that's a good one. We'll celebrate that with you. Aye, here's to travels in outer space.'

I ripped the bags open one after the other and stuffed the crisps into my mouth.

'Had they no crisps in outer space?' Kenny joked, and the locals laughed again.

I gulped half the first pint down in one go and crammed down the peanuts so quickly, I was lucky not to choke. As I washed them down with the second pint, my eyes were drawn to the news on TV. I sat riveted, waiting to see if there would be more news about abductions, but the lads at the bar were more interested in football.

Kenny changed the channel to a Gaelic match.

'What day is it?' I asked him.

'Thursday.'

'And the date?'

'The fourteenth.'

It didn't help. I looked at the calendar behind the bar. The year was still 2025. That didn't make sense.

Kenny told me that the police had found my car abandoned by the side of the road and had moved it to the hotel car park. He went on to say that he had the keys to it and that I'd better phone the police immediately.

I needed to be alone to think.

Is it possible that hardly any time's passed?

'Can I get a room, and can you put the pints on my tab?'

'What, no cashpoints on the planet ZOG?' he chuckled, handing me a room key.

I collected my travelling bag and made my way unsteadily up to the room where I sat head in hands on the bed.

How could I have been away for only four days? It makes absolutely no sense.

I showered and shaved, staring at my reflection in the mirror. It didn't seem any different to me than the one that I had left Earth with. My hair had recently been cut and the potbelly I'd managed to put back on after all the celebrations of my freedom appeared to have vanished. I looked the same as the day I had been taken.

With a trembling finger, I dialled Isabel from the room landline.

I swallowed. 'Isabel … it's me.'

'Paddy, where were you?'

Her voice sounded both relieved and annoyed, but I was so happy to hear it.

I tried to clear the croak in my voice, believing it best to tell her a white lie, saying that I'd had to go out to an emergency on an oil rig and was out on a cliff walk when the response team picked me up. That was why my car had been abandoned. I wasn't going to tell her the truth over the phone and have her think I'd lost my mind.

'Did you lose your phone as well?' I didn't answer. 'Did the whole rig lose communications? You usually call me every night, so …'

I still said nothing, my mind working overtime, heart thumping. But she was still staring, her accusatory eyes burning into me. Eventually, I came up with something half credible. 'I wasn't expecting to get picked up and my phone battery went flat on the walk. You know how it is when a phone's constantly trying to connect and there's no signal. It runs the battery flat in no time. Anyway, the boss was supposed to call you while I was en route. You mean he forgot? Dozy bastard!'

'What day is today?' she asked in a cool voice, having let that point go and she was now moving on to the next thing to moan about. Hardly surprising.

'It's Thursday,' I said.

'Thursday, the what?'

'Thursday the fourteenth of February.'

'Does that date mean … anything to you?' she asked. The cool tone had turned icy.

'Yes,' I said meekly, 'It's Valentine's Day. And the anniversary of the day we met.'

'Correct,' she said. 'And all the other women I know got flowers and chocolates today. And where is my husband? Missing for the week and then too busy to call.'

She hung up.

It wasn't my fault that I'd been abducted, was it?

There I was, a short time earlier delighted to be home, and now I was being forced to seriously question my sanity. But then, if I had dreamt up the whole episode, how could I explain the spacesuit and Nobby?

I went to where my car had been left, picked up my case and returned to the room where I changed into regular clothes. I made Nobby up a comfortable bed.

Then, I headed back down, this time to the restaurant. I hadn't had a real meal with anything I could identify since God only knew when. The fish was always good in the Western Strands, being so close to the Atlantic Ocean, and fish I had definitely not eaten in my travels, so choosing the fish casserole was a no-brainer.

As I sat waiting at the dining table with the knife and fork in my hand, I stared at other people's plates, watching them lift their forks to their mouths, and imagined the food slowly making its way down their throats. The aroma made me drool.

After what seemed like an everlasting wait, the meal arrived. The casserole came in a wide, deep bowl, and beside it on a plate were jacket potatoes, string beans and carrots. With my spoon, I lifted out a soup-drenched shrimp, chewed it, and it slid down my throat like silk. The soup abounded with spices and herbs and danced on my tongue. No time to waste, I lifted a jacket potato, deciding not to peel it, and dunked it into the bowl. The highlight of the hotpot was a large portion of smoked cod.

I tore pieces from it with my fork, mixing it with potatoes, vegetables and soup until the last morsel was gone. I'd had some first class meals in my time, but that was the most memorable one.

I called to the waitress. 'Compliments to the chef, and could I have the same again with a bottle of Rioja, please?'

After two pints, five packets of crisps and peanuts, two dinners and a bottle of wine, I was well ready for bed. Exhausted, I slept soundly.

***

For breakfast, a full Irish was on the menu. Sausage, bacon, black-and-white pudding, fried eggs … *To hell with animal rights, this is far too tasty.*

Having dealt with the massive fry-up, I walked to the Belmullet police station to report my abduction. Did they know about the Rapture, I asked?

They nodded. But still, they stared blankly when I told them it had happened to me. No other person in the whole of Ireland had been reported missing since the Rapture had begun, and no other person in the world had reported they had made it back.

I sat in a chair across a desk from two straight-faced uniformed officers, one typing and the other asking questions. They thought I hadn't noticed when they rolled eyes at each other as I related my story from the moment of abandoning the car at Erris Head.

When, in response to their request, they received a full description of the aliens that had abducted me, they lost their composure, bursting into laughter.

I signed the report and left, embarrassed, their guffaws following me down the steps.

Somewhat humiliated and chastened, I phoned work to explain that I had been abducted by aliens and needed at least a week off to convalesce.

'I've heard it all now!' the plant manager said when he'd eventually stopped laughing. Following such an outlandish excuse, however, he did agree to it.

Chapter 17: Home, Sweet Home

Isabel was admiring her front garden flowerbeds when I pulled into the driveway, then rushed from the car to embrace her heavily pregnant form.

But she fended me off, hardly able to spare me a look.

Katie and Ana Marje, our two youngest, burst out of the front door.

I lifted them both at the same time, hugging and kissing them. An immense feeling of love for them swept through me as I held them.

'The police were here! Where were you, Dad?'

'I had to rush away and didn't have time to tell anyone. Some idiot at work forgot to tell your mam.' This was the easiest excuse.

As soon as I returned them to the ground, they jumped up and down, wanting to know if I had brought them a gift as usual.

'Well, where I've been, they didn't have anything for children your size ... But what I did get you is ... well, come and see!'

They skipped behind me to the car. I lifted Nobby out and put her on the ground. They squealed in utter delight, the kind of noise only two little girls can make.

Our labrador retriever, Ranger, came to meet tiny Nobby.

He was normally a friendly dog, but he greeted this odd-looking newcomer with a vicious and territorial snarl, making Nobby duck her head and run under the car.

We put Ranger in the house, and I enticed Nobby to come back out.

'Are you sure that's a dog?' Katie asked. 'With that funny mane? And why is Ranger behaving really weird?'

'Is it a pup? How old is it?' Ana asked.

'No, she's not a pup anymore. I don't know when a pup becomes a dog, but she's still young, I guess.' I lifted Nobby and stroked her back.

Ranger was allowed back out and I let them sniff each other. When we noticed they were both wagging their tails, I let Nobby down so they could make friends.

***

That evening, Isabel cooked a roast chicken for dinner.

She was quiet at the table as we ate.

I talked to the children and after I'd put them to bed, I sat back at the dining table, ready for the inquisition.

Her impatience was obvious in her tightening frown.

I told her my story.

'Ha!' she scoffed. 'Well, I have to say, that is the most outrageous excuse for forgetting Valentine's Day. Strangely enough though,' she said, 'I did have a dream, that you were with another woman.' She glared at me. 'Were you?'

I was never a liar, and above all, would never tell a lie to Isabel. Not knowing what to say, I said nothing. The seconds passed.

'I'll ask again. Were you with another woman, up in Mayo?'

'No! You're the only woman I have ever loved anywhere on Earth.'

'Then, tell me the truth, this time … About where you were and how come you forgot your pregnant wife on Valentine's Day?'

'You have to believe me! What about the animal I brought home? Have you ever seen a dog like that before?'

'No,' she conceded. 'But it looks like a cross between a sheep and a dog—and you wouldn't know what would be going on in the hills in Mayo.'

'Down, Nobby! Down!' I ordered Nobby down from the arm of the chair where she was sitting, staring at Isabel.

Since arriving at the house Nobby had been following Isabel everywhere and when she stopped, Nobby would also stop, and then just stare at her.

'Must that dog stare at me all the time?' Isabel complained. 'What is so fascinating about me? What is it? Am I some sort of canine enigma? Does the dog know something I don't? It's creepy. I feel stalked and hounded. No pun intended.'

'Ranger is from another planet. This whole experience is new to her. I guess that's why …' I offered. 'I wish you would believe me.'

'I'd like to, Paddy, but you know what I think? It's more likely you drank too much poteen with the locals in some shebeen in the middle of nowhere.' She gave a sour laugh. 'But I suppose Rapture is unexplained. I'll sleep on it. You're forgiven, so long as you come to bed right now.'

We hugged and went to bed.

***

That week, I scoured for news of new abductions, but the last reported instance had been on the 12th of February, over a week ago. I felt alone in this world with my story. Surely no one else had made it back? My mind soon went to Tom and the others.

I didn't have enough information to track down their families, and even if I had, would they have believed me if I'd told them their father and husband had been eaten, devoured by leprechauns on a planet lightyears away?

After my purported sick leave, it was time to go back to work. As usual, the alarm went off at 5:00 a.m., waking us both. It was momentarily surreal, a *normal* day back in *normal* territory on 'my' planet, being woken at some ridiculous hour to resume a life that—literally—had been lightyears away until not so long ago.

Isabel asked me to stay in bed, but I had to get to work.

So, in the coldness of the morning, I reluctantly got up, washing and dressing, making my usual tea in my travel mug. On opening the front door, it was pitch dark.

The sky was moonless and without stars. I started the car, turning on the headlamps, relieved to note that at least the road conditions were good this morning.

After a long five-hour drive, I approached Erris Head with great trepidation, finally happy to see no sign of the Northern Lights. In the office, my story had already been broadcast throughout the entire plant, sceptical colleagues crowding around, some grinning, some serious, asking about my 'adventure' and making 'alien' sounds.

I promised I would tell them over a pint, which I later did, but only a short version.

They would not believe me anyway.

As with all engineering projects, there were strict deadlines to be met, and it was not long before we were all concentrating on the work in hand and my story was forgotten.

That week went quickly and so did the following two. As the days passed, the thought that I had been abducted became less and less real to me too.

I was utterly preoccupied with the anticipation of the imminent birth.

What would the new twins' life bring to us and them?

I hoped my memories from the galaxies were some sort of bizarre dream.

As I drove home that Friday afternoon, I got a call. Isabel was going into labour.

Luckily, I arrived in plenty of time to see her safely deliver two healthy and strong babies that evening, a boy and a girl. We cradled and admired each one as we passed them between us, both so overcome with joy, so deliriously happy too.

Isabel looked tired but contented to have overcome this great challenge.

The nurse took the babies from us, and I held Isabel's hand as she drifted off for a much-needed sleep, a warm glow washing over me. I knew this feeling. It was the same I'd had with our other children, this love familiar and unmistakable.

After the euphoria of the birth had subsided, the twins arrived home and settled in. They were the sweetest babies ever, and everybody wanted to see them.

One of the first visitors to the house was Nobby … the human one. Someday soon, I looked forward to him being introduced to his alien dog namesake.

After congratulating us on the twins and going all wide-eyed and emotional at the news that I'd named the pup after him, Nobby told me that his mother was asking for me. We arranged that once the babies had settled, I would go to his house to see her.

Afterwards, Nobby and I would go for a pint to catch up.

Chapter 18: Nobby, the Human

After we had returned from Australia, Nobby got a job with an American multi-national computer company as a salesman and was repeatedly named Salesman of the Year. He had continued to study and then got a master's degree in marketing.

He'd made a great success of his career, quickly climbing the ranks to eventually becoming the CEO of the Irish branch.

He was now living in a beautiful Georgian house on the hill of Howth.

I walked up the driveway, admiring it and also the mews alongside, in which his mother lived. Beside the house was a large field with stables for his children's ponies.

His beautiful wife, Sinead, answered the door. 'Come in,' she said.

I was immediately struck by the height of the woman. As she stood there in front of me, she seemed so tall that she would have looked more in place standing beside me.

'Look who's here!' she announced as I entered the sitting room.

Nobby was sitting in an armchair reading the paper, wearing his slippers. Looking up, he whipped off his glasses and jumped up as if something had bitten him.

'Come down here,' he said and opened his arms. We hugged for a few seconds and then he lifted his hand for a high five and a knuckle-punch.

'I told Mam you were coming, and she's dying to see you. I'd better bring you straight out to her.'

Mrs Soft was leaning back in a big, black, leather automated chair. At the push of a button, it tilted upright. I walked over and kissed her on the cheek.

'How are you, Mrs Soft?'

'Oh, I'm very well, but very tired now, you know. I've been spreading pony manure in the garden since I got up. Hard work is the only way I can get a good night's sleep.'

She put her iPad down on the coffee table beside her. She was a thoroughly modern tech-savvy eighty-seven-year-old woman, conversant with all the latest gadgets and apps. This helped her keep in touch with the many people she had met and friends she had made throughout her life. She was in as regular contact with the people she had known decades ago—from the time she'd worked as a part-time waitress in the Towers—as with those she had met later through playing bridge and grass bowling.

'Where are you working now, Paddy?' she asked.

She knew I often worked on projects leading me to travel.

'In Belmullet in Mayo, working on a new gas terminal project.'

'Oh yes. I've seen on the TV, all those violent protests and rioting with all the police involvement. I'm surprised I didn't see *you* on television too, right in the middle of it.'

She smiled.

I grinned back.

Sinead had cooked us a beautiful roast lamb dinner.

Nobby carved, and the three teenagers—Trudy the eldest, Margaret and Norbert og means *young* in Irish—each played their part in serving the meal. We sat down together around a large round table. They excitedly told me about their ponies and their participation in the upcoming Dublin Horse Show. Then, the conversation turned to their dogs, and especially to the extra-large

Alsatian which they'd found as a starving stray. Their Dad, they said, had insisted he be called Paddy, after me.

I laughed. 'That's a real coincidence because I found the tiniest labrador-ish pup, and called her Nobby, after your dad!'

I showed them photos, in one of which Nobby the dog was asleep on my foot. They noticed her mane, commenting it was the strangest dog they had ever seen.

'She's a funny looking thing. Where did you get her?' they wanted to know.

'Aye, bit of a runt. A farmer in Mayo gave her to me.'

It was a delicious meal. Their standards hadn't changed since the first time I had eaten dinner in the Towers all those years ago. The conversation flowed until Nobby announced the two of us were heading out for pints.

Mrs Soft straightened in her chair, asking the children to go out to the kitchen and start on the dishes. When they'd left the room, she turned to Sinead.

'Don't let the two of them out together, Sinead. They attract trouble.'

Sinead, a voice of sense and reason, said, 'Now, Grandma, I know the two of them were a bit wild in their day, but they'll have calmed down now they're in their fifties.'

'Well, so you say, Sinead. But I always will worry about Norbert when he goes out with Paddy. Something just happens. It always docs. It's like putting a match to the fuse on a stick of dynamite. You just wait and see.'

'Mam, don't worry! We're only going to the pub for a few pints. What could possibly happen? Don't you think you're exaggerating a bit?'

'Would you not rather stay home, love, and have a drink in the conservatory? What's the difference? There's loads of Guinness and whiskey there.

'Mam, we're going out. We've not been out together for a long time.'

'Right. And 'going out' means trouble, I know it does because the only thing you can do 'out' that you can't do in your own home is make a nuisance of yourselves. I won't sleep a wink until you're home,' she said with a sad, troubled face.

***

We arrived at Tommy Byrne's at about 9 p.m. The time in the taxi from Howth to Dublin City centre allowed us to digest the fine meal, and we were ready to drink many pints. The barman instantly recognised us, and as we sat on high stools at the bar, two creamy pints of Guinness arrived.

We both took deep draughts of the ebony elixir.

'Right, so, what is it you wanted to talk to me about?' Nobby enquired.

I took a breath, launching into a brief version of my story.

He sat listening, agog, and when I'd finished my tale, seconds passed.

Then he asked, 'Paddy, did you get another thumping like you got in Australia by any chance? That story's even better than meeting St. Peter and your grandmother at the Pearly Gates.'

'No, Nobby. Aliens got hold of me and beat me up this time. I went missing for four days and arrived back to the Western Strands Hotel bar, dressed in maroon boxer shorts over a bizarre orange onesie. And not only that, but I was with a tiny dog, the likes of which this world has never seen before. This cannot be explained simply by putting it down to a few knocks on the head! And I'm looking to you for advice.'

Grinning, he said, 'Sounds to me like a construction party that got completely out of order. The mountain poteen mustn't have been distilled properly; that can happen and drive people scatty. Somebody may have put magic mushrooms in your stew, who knows? And as for you arriving back in the hotel in somebody else's boxer shorts, I don't even want to imagine how that happened!' He couldn't keep himself from laughing. 'Did you check with the other construction workers? Did any of *them* go to outer space and come back in the wrong underpants?'

His smile faded at my stony, straight face. 'Anyway, what's your question?'

'Do I go public with the story or not?'

In his haste to answer me and swallow at the same time, he started coughing and choking on his pint. 'No, don't. What would be the point of doing that, pal? You've no real proof, and you'd be a laughingstock if you told such a weird story.'

'But Nobby, you know others have risen. It's been all over the news. Aliens fishing for food … It's no weirder than the idea of the Rapture.'

Nobby listened, frowning.

'I mean, think of it, the pre-Tribulation Rapture written in the Bible's book of apocalypse, the final seven years of this age. True followers of Jesus Christ being transformed into their spiritual bodies and taken from the Earth to be in Heaven with God. Non-believers left behind to face severe tribulation as the antichrist prepares to take his place. So which story is weirder—theirs or mine?'

Nobby looked uncomfortable. He ordered more pints as if that solved everything.

I pushed on. 'People have been believing the Rapture story for thousands of years, and it might yet be true. My point is that I was abducted and would have been slaughtered and eaten if that kid hadn't bought me at the auction. Diaz sends fleets of spaceships cruising the galaxies looking for food. Diazians themselves look like leprechauns, which everybody in the world believes are a myth, but they're extra-terrestrials that arrived in Ireland tens of thousands of years ago.'

My voice had become impassioned, and Nobby was looking increasingly uncomfortable. 'OK, Paddy. If all that's true, how come you're back safely on Earth?'

'Because they judged me to be innocent and sent me back to teach the rest of the humans to respect animals in our care.'

'Would you *stop!*' said Nobby. 'Look who's talking—the man who has just devoured a huge plate of lamb!'

'Yeah, but cattle and sheep live naturally in fields. If we didn't eat them, wolves or dogs would. That's nature's way. Look, Nobby, I'm not talking about the cattle we see roaming in the fields, I'm talking about confined pigs and chickens that never see the light of day. Just look around at all the chicken wings and pork spareribs. People don't realise the suffering that went on behind the meat they're enjoying.'

Nobby raised his glass.

'My good friend, I agree. You couldn't keep dogs or ponies in such a way, so who said it's acceptable to make the lives of pigs and chickens a living hell, so people can enjoy cheaper meat?'

There was silence for a moment. Then Nobby downed another gulp of Guinness.

'You know, Paddy, free-range meat is leaner and healthier, with lower cholesterol. It's a win-win situation for the consumer and the animals. The meat would be only pennies more expensive, so we might just need to eat slightly less. Looking around the bellies in this bar, that would be a good thing. Ireland could become a world leader in animal rights and food quality. Remember how we led the way with our smoking ban and much of the rest of the world followed our example?'

I felt extremely uncomfortable with what I was about to say, shrinking slightly as I said it. 'The big problem's always been that I'm a coward. I don't have the guts. It's all very easy getting you on side. But to stand up and persuade the world it's all out of step is quite another thing.'

'You, a *coward?'* Nobby challenged. 'Never seen you take a step backwards. Ever.'

'I'm big, strong, and good with my fists, so it's easy to stand my ground when it comes to brawling, but this is different. I'm a *moral* coward. I don't have the courage to give my opinion on something controversial if people might laugh at me or talk about me behind my back. I can't negotiate, can't talk my way out of a situation. All I can ever do is say, 'You're one ugly bastard!' and then hit them. The brave people in the world are people like Greta Thunberg who selflessly give themselves to a cause.

I couldn't go over to talk to your man and his friends over there eating chicken wings and ask them to eat only free-range wings in future …'

'You couldn't? Why not? Not that I'm advocating you should either.'

'Like I said, I wouldn't do it in case they laugh at me.'

Nobby looked ever so slightly bemused.

'Well, I'm glad you're not going to do it anyway, or we'd end up in a brawl just as my mother predicted!' He looked up to the ceiling. 'By the way, what happened to that fun-loving guy who was always great company? Ooh, I forgot, he's down on himself because he's just back from outer space and on a mission to save all the world's factory farmed animals. But he can't because he's a moral chicken himself.' Nobby grinned. *'I* know what you need.'

He ordered two whiskeys.

'Sláinte!'

We knocked our glasses together and downed the whiskey. I ordered another two for the road. Suitably fortified, we were just about ready to leave the cosy haven of the pub. Outside, it was lashing with rain.

'It's going to be hard to get a taxi,' I said.

'Yeah, I know. Let's get a tricycle instead,' he shouted, running into the street to hail one. 'Come on!' he yelled, and I ran to get into the tricycle taxi with him.

'Where are we going in this thing?' I laughed. 'We needed a taxi. This won't get us home!'

'Home? We're not going home. We're going to Buckler's!'

'Buckler's nightclub! Are you mad? We haven't been there for decades.'

'Yeah, that's about right, and that's why it's a great idea to go now.'

***

We arrived at Buckler's and who was at the door but a face from our distant past, Ronnie.

'I can't believe my eyes … it's Paddy and Nobby!' he said. 'I haven't seen you guys in years!'

We made our way through the nightclub's writhing, massed throng which was at fever pitch, to the garden bar.

Nobby ordered an expensive bottle of 2005 Châteauneuf-du-Pape.

I sat on a bar stool and Nobby remained standing.

With the deafening bass *thump-thump* of the music, it was the only way we could be at the same ear level to hear each other. We were laughing about the times we had spent together, when somebody pushed up against me.

Too busy talking to pay much heed, I gave a cursory glance over my shoulder, noticing a girl with black hair. *Considering the length of this bar, why is she pushing up to me?* I thought nothing more of it, but when we went to refill our glasses, our wine bottle was gone. Looking around, I saw the girl sitting on her own at a nearby booth designed for six people. Her eyes fixed on me.

In stark contrast to her jet black, straight, long hair, she possessed very pale skin. Her lips were vivid with blood-red lipstick. She wore dark eye shadow and—proudly—a Celtic-style neck tattoo which extended to her breasts; those were barely covered by a very tight, skimpy, sleeveless top. To complete the ensemble, she wore tight leather pants and *Pirates of the Caribbean*-style high-heeled boots. The fact she had probably taken the wine seemed bizarrely apt under the circumstances.

'Just investigating the whereabouts of our wine,' I said to Nobby, making my way over to the booth. Lifting a half-empty bottle of Châteauneuf-du-Pape that looked suspiciously like ours, I read the label aloud. '2005. Now that is a very good year and a real coincidence.' I topped up her glass. 'Would this be my bottle of wine, and if so, could I please have it back? Even if a lot of it seems to have evaporated …'

'Aw, you're not going to take it away now, are you? I was hoping you'd sit with me. I'm the sort of woman who doesn't like to be disappointed. I'm a queen, don't you know? Let me introduce myself. I'm Grainne O'Malley, direct descendant and namesake of Ireland's pirate and warrior queen from the sixteenth century.'

She held out her hand for me to kiss which I politely did.

'You may have heard of my father, Flat Cap O'Malley? He's often in the news; he runs Dublin's underworld.'

I was initially too astonished to speak.

Then I summoned a little composure and the barest scattering of words.

'I'd really love to join you, but unfortunately, my wife wouldn't let me.'

It sounded so lame, something evident the second it escaped my mouth.

'What height are you, big boy?'

'Six feet, eight inches tall,' I replied.

'Wow! Tell me, are you built in proportion?'

'If I was, I'd be eight feet, six inches,' I said, laughing.

I hoped she'd see the funny side too, so we could part company, no damage done.

'How dare you defy me by not joining me as I have summoned you to?'

Clearly, she *hadn't* seen the funny side. Or was she pulling my leg? Probably.

Anyway, I took the wine bottle and went back to Nobby.

'That girl is seriously nuts. Let's go inside and finish our wine,' I suggested.

We were standing between dance floor and bar when a fellow departed the garden bar, rushing straight towards me. I assumed this character to be one of her henchmen.

Without a word, he jumped up and wrapped his legs around my waist, then clasped his hands around the back of my neck. His head tilted back. I knew his intention was to launch forward with a head butt.

I caught my hands under his knees then lifting them up. His grip on the back of my neck slipped, and I turned him upside down the perfect rugby spear tackle.

'You're one ugly bastard!' I yelled.

He landed directly on his head before ending up on his back.

I thought I may have broken his neck, seeing him lying still on the ground.

He was out for the count.

Then, he was back on his feet just as fast!

I squared up to him and he retreated to where he'd come from.

Nobby looked nervous. 'Do you think we should just drink up and go?'

Whilst we were draining our glasses at the bar, a punch landed on my jaw. My assailant was back with his friends again.

Nobby grabbed the glass from my hand as I let fly with a quick succession of jabs, a left, right, left, and the man was on his back on the floor again.

Then, his friends started throwing punches.

Nobby and I knew exactly what to do.

I stepped back and picked my punches, and as I did so, Nobby finished them off from below. It was just like old times.

The bouncers intervened and graciously led us to the exit.

Ronnie was there and told us to scarper. Since we were twenty-five years older than our assailants, he wanted to give us a good head start before he'd throw the others out.

We ran as fast as we could down the street until we met the canal towpath along which we continued our escape. Here, we were able to slow the pace slightly and catch our breath. When we could run no further, we walked under streetlights to the next bridge and returned to the main road, where we could get a taxi.

Then we saw it, an unpassable late-night venue, the 'Howl at the Moon' diner.

Taking one look at each other, we knew we were thinking the same thing and headed straight for it. They were just closing, but we managed to sneak in, hastily ordering two house special burgers with fries and then sitting at an uncleared table.

Here, we were confronted by a whole bowl of chicken wings left untouched, imploring us to eat them. We both drooled over them, then stared at each other.

Nobby spoke first. 'I know we agreed a few hours ago never to eat chicken wings again but this is a special circumstance.'

'How so?' I asked.

'Well, the chickens have already lived their horrible lives and died their horrible deaths. We agree on that. We did not even order them, and they're about to go to waste. They have shown up on our table, and if we don't eat them, they'll be thrown in the bin. So, we might as well eat them. Waste not, want not. It'd be obscene to say no.'

I was starving, so didn't question his logic, and we both tucked in. As we were wiping our mouths and cleaning our hands, the manager came over.

'Did you guys order and pay for those wings?' he asked.

We explained that we had ordered what we wanted and then when we sat at the table, discovered that somebody had left them behind.

So we thought there was no harm in eating them. 'How much are they?' I enquired, fumbling for change in my pocket. 'Here, let me pay it.'

He then gave a blank look and left us, never waiting to accept any cash.

As we waited for our burgers, a police car arrived, lights flashing. We questioned why they were there.

'Must be a fight somewhere, Bucklers was too far away so nothing to do with us. Seems quiet enough though, doesn't it?'

The particular question of why the police had turned up was soon answered when we had two officers along with the manager standing next to our table.

'These are the two gombeens who stole from my restaurant,' the manager said, jabbing his finger at the two of us.

Nobby's eye was blackening, and my jaw hurt.

'Looks like they've been fighting too,' said one officer to the other. 'A night in a cell will cool these hooligans off.'

We never even got to eat our paid-for burgers before they arrested us, bringing us to the station for questioning.

We told the guards about being assaulted in Buckler's and once they confirmed our identification, we were free to leave.

We got into a taxi.

Nobby's eye was now fully black.

'Sorry about that, Nobby.'

'No bother. It wasn't your fault.'

'It *was* my fault. We got into a fight.'

'Well, it was my fault for bringing you to Buckler's, and it was me who suggested eating the wings.'

We agreed that the two of us together, in certain situations, was a recipe invariably leading to disaster.

'Don't tell your ma!' I joked, exiting the taxi. 'I think she's psychic …'

Nobby laughed and continued his journey home to Howth.

***

All the family were fast asleep when I got home so I snuck up the stairs and slid into bed without waking Isabel.

Later, when I woke, she was downstairs tending to the children.

I made my way to the bathroom, relieved myself of my full bladder from the night before, and leaned on the sink to survey my face in the mirror.

It was evident that I'd been fighting, and my jaw hurt.

What sort of a night was that?

All I'd wanted to do was talk something out with an old friend. *But oh, no. Not you! That is not the way it works for you, is it, Paddy, my lad?*

My thoughts raced back to the time I had been acquitted on Diaz and to the subsequent mission given to me. *Return to Earth and do your utmost to educate fellow humans on bringing an end to intensive farming …* And here I was, about to face criminal charges for stealing somebody else's caged, leftover chicken wings!

And then there was the matter of getting involved in a punch up with Dublin's top criminal gang. *Oh God!* As I looked in the bathroom mirror, I could barely suppress a severe bout of self-loathing. I felt thoroughly ashamed, but would have to tell the whole story to Isabel. She was the calmest, most understanding person you could meet, but her composure was tested on hearing about the previous evening.

'First, you are apparently abducted by aliens, and now this! And you, with two beautiful new babies to look after!'

I hadn't seen her this cross before.

She sat seething with anger, refusing to speak to me and could hardly spare me a glance. A good night's sleep cures all were one of her mantra's, she was back to her calm and serene self after a few of them

Soon afterwards, I was very happy to hear that my part in the project in Mayo had come to an end and I was being transferred back to Dublin.

Isabel was relieved to have me there to help with the babies.

Working in Dublin meant no more getting up in the small hours of the morning and I could finish work early at every opportunity.

One evening, I had fed and changed the twins, and with a sleeping baby cradled in each arm, I watched David Attenborough's *Blue Planet* on television.

The documentary brought it all home to me: Earth was being destroyed.

My trial, Polpus' accusations, the inconvenient truth that I wanted to pass off as a terrible dream, was in fact reality. My heart sank.

What sort of a world had I brought these sweetest of babies into? It was a wake-up call, one that stunned me. I had to do something.

Chapter 19: Cosmological Prodigy

I went to watch Kevin playing rugby, taking Ranger and Nobby on their leads.

A radio host from a national broadcasting station was watching the game beside me; fascinated by Nobby, he asked what breed of dog it was and where I had got it from. These were questions I was hearing almost daily by now.

I told of how I'd come by her, no longer making up the lie that I'd got her from a farmer. What was the point? He looked as if he wished he hadn't asked, but a dog with a mane seemed too intriguing. Laughing, he told me his name was Joe.

'That's hell of a story you just told me there, Paddy,' he voiced. 'Whether it has an ounce of truth is for you to know and for me to guess. I don't suppose you'd be interested in telling it to listeners on my radio show, would you?'

I agreed to tell it over the phone two weeks later, on a show called *Live Line*.

As the days passed, my feet grew colder and colder about going on air.

Nobody had believed me up to that point, so why would Joe's listeners be any different? In the end, I resolved that it was my duty, no matter what.

On the day itself, however, as the hour of the broadcast approached, I was seriously regretting volunteering, not wanting the whole nation laughing at me. I hadn't told anybody that I was going to be interviewed. I left the office, walking to a quiet park bench where I sat down on a bench with a bottle of water, my throat dry.

My phone said 3:05 p.m., and Live Line began at 3 p.m. I pleaded with my phone not to ring. But it eventually did.

'Is that Paddy O'Reilly?'

'It is.'

'You wanted to tell your story about being abducted by aliens?'

'I do.'

'I'm putting you through to Joe, now.'

'Grand, so.'

When Joe introduced me, I jumped up from the bench and paced up and down, beginning to tell my story.

I started at the beginning because there was no other place to begin, describing the snowy, dark morning, the weird lights and being lifted off my feet, ascending.

I shared with him how scared I had been and how it had felt like I was going to die.

Joe knew what he was doing as an experienced, accomplished anchor and radio host, putting me at ease and even trying to empathise with me as much as he could.

I lost my nervousness, talking animatedly about the Greys, the food and the condition of the pens where we'd been kept. I talked about the failed rebellion.

At first, it all seemed plausible—after all, it had only been a few months since the mysterious Rapture disappearances.

But when, with all of Ireland listening, I got to my experience with the human-eating leprechauns, and then the vegetarian leprechauns who'd returned me to Earth to convince humans to improve animal welfare, it all seemed to become too far-fetched.

It may have been only my imagination and heightened sensitivity, but something was telling me the leprechauns had been a step too far.

As if to support that theory, Joe cleared his throat, wished me good luck, and swiftly wrapped up the conversation, moving on to the next caller.

***

After that, I couldn't walk down the street without people pointing and laughing.

I had not only embarrassed myself but also, my whole family.

Even Nobby phoned, complaining. 'I told you not to go public with that weird story, because you've no proof. Now look at what you've done! We'll be a laughingstock!'

I felt ashamed, but Isabel wasn't. She stood by me, admitting she hadn't believed me in the beginning, but there was evidence, my spacesuit and a peculiar little dog with a mane, yet to be explained. She told me to walk tall, stand straight.

'Once you do, you're unbeatable. The prison most people live in is worrying about what other's think,' she declared sagely.

I bore no bad memories about what had happened, getting accustomed to the ridicule. In many ways, that radio interview was a gift because it was controversial, and though some people laughed, some others believed me. My story became topical and with that notoriety, I was soon invited on to the Irish *Late, Late Show*.

This time, I had prepared ahead and when the host introduced me, I came out in my orange space onesie. Though my head was encased, I could still see well enough to walk over to the host, Mick O'Toole, who remarked on the uniqueness of my attire.

I sat down, peeled back the suit to expose my head and told the audience that this was what I'd been wearing upon returning from the galaxies.

The audience thought this was a joke, laughing, and then Mick said, 'They're not laughing *with* you. They're laughing *at* you.'

Ignoring his remark, I began to demonstrate how the onesie had been constructed. I pulled back the head covering, and it shrank back inside the body of the suit.

Then I walked onto the centre of the stage and showed the cameras that there were no seams, zips or Velcro. I demonstrated to the audience exactly how it worked, how to take it off by starting to peel it back and allowing it to continue to peel by itself.

I explained that the suit was designed to protect the wearer from any extremes of temperature or pressure which might be encountered in space.

To prepare for the show, I had also left the suit for some time with the Dublin Institute for Technology. The professor who had examined it was in the audience and he came to stand on stage beside me, confirming that, though the investigation was ongoing, their findings to date had shown that the technology used to make the suit was not, to their knowledge, available on this planet.

In short, we had nothing like this, he said.

Now I had the audience's attention, continuing to give them the whole story of my abduction. To finish on a light note, I mimicked the reactions of the people as I'd walked into the Western Strand bar with Nobby under my arm.

This got the audience laughing. They hadn't known what to believe until now, but this scene, they could picture clearly, and it seemed to endear them.

'Does anybody want to meet Nobby?' I asked, and with that, Isabel led her out from the wings. I sat back down and lifted her up onto my lap, stroking her and showing off her mane. The audience appeared captivated, but as I looked out at them, there still seemed to be a lot of sceptical faces, many looking as if they were ridiculing me.

A zoologist from Dublin Zoo had also been invited into the audience. Just as the materials technologist had done with the flight suit, he confirmed that after examining Nobby, he was convinced there no breed of Earth dog held the same DNA as hers.

Then I went on to explain how I had been responsible for the ceasing of the Rapture, continuing that we were still being watched by intellectually superior beings who considered humans a very low life form. Furthermore, if we didn't start to treat the animals in our care with the respect they deserved, the Rapture would return, and we'd be treated in the same way we treated factory-farmed animals.

'And then they will eat us,'

***

My appearance on the show sparked more conversation about my story, the video circulating around Ireland. In a short space of time, the film went viral with many million viewers worldwide.

Some people put my story down to more evidence of extra-terrestrial encounters. Others believed it to be an elaborate hoax, and yet more just dismissed me as a nutcase.

What more evidence could the public need to believe me? I thought.

After a few weeks, the story had been consigned to yesterday's news recycling bin.

***

I went for a long walk down to Bull Island, a beach nearby. From the water's edge, I watched dark clouds gather. A strong wind was blowing, waves rolling in from the swell of the distant storm. The wind was lifting the sand and carrying it up to waist level. *How unusual*, I thought, continuing walking, enjoying the sight.

A great, dramatic storm seemed to be fermenting. Despite the fact that it was mid-afternoon, savage forked lightning lit up the darkening sky. In the distance, a ball of light shot across the sky and then hovered, stationary, just above me.

In an instant, a woman about 6'2" and wearing a red skin-tight catsuit was standing in front of me. 'Paddy, it's me, Arielle!'

No, no! I can't take any more. I thought my life had returned to normal. *Wake up, wake up, Paddy!* I pleaded with myself. *This must be a dream. Or is it?*

'Arielle, is it yourself, sweetheart? I can't believe it's you!'

'How come you have become so tall?'

'I love you, and want to be perfect for you, so I researched that women are generally about six inches shorter than men on earth. I got cosmetic surgery so we would be a couple of average height if we stand together, so people won't take any notice of me.'

I could not fault her logic. Neither could I stop myself from staring in admiration at this version of Arielle, with her buxom, yet otherwise slim physique and her hair like golden corn at harvest time. Her complexion was exotic. Crimson, full lips oozed lusciousness, while high cheekbones accentuated her perfection.

Oh, they would notice you all right! Who would be able to keep their eyes off you … a goddess more beautiful than a cosmopolitan film star?

'Why have you come here?' I asked.

Looking into my eyes, she spoke softly. 'I love you and have missed you so much that I have come to be with you, to guard, guide, and help you.'

'Help me? That's so nice of you! But if Isabel finds out I'm married to you, I'm done for.'

'My love, we will have to let her know.'

I must have looked nonplussed, caught unawares, robbed of all words.

She had more to say. 'Diazian alpha directive forbids contact with more primitive civilizations, but we have been covertly observing this planet. Humans are not morally enlightened in a way that is necessary to keep up with their advancing technology. So, I volunteered to help. As I say, I can guide you.'

The ball of light which had shone down from above extinguished itself.

The storm subsided, the dark clouds parting.

I stood back in awe, in the presence of a perfectly formed woman, a goddess with unsurpassed beauty.

The waist-high sandstorm passed too, everything perfectly still and calm again.

'Where, and for how long, do you intend to stay?' I enquired.

'I will stay with you, of course, forever. I looked after you in Diaz, and we are married so I will look after you here also.'

'Yes, I know that you looked after me before, but that was then, and up there … and while I'm married to you on Diaz, I'm married to Isabel here on Earth. I have a four-bedroomed house. Our rooms are full. We have kids. Where do you intend sleeping?'

'With you,' she replied.

'I sleep with Isabel.'

'I'll sleep with the two of you then.'

'Would you stop! I've got myself in enough trouble with Isabel recently; she would be very annoyed if I told her that she had to share our bed with another woman, oh, and by the way, the other woman is my wife from another planet! No, no. Forget that. You are not staying in my house. I'll have to book you into a hotel for the moment.'

I looked at all her luggage.

Those Diazian pilots are useless!

First, they dropped me off on a ledge in the middle of nowhere, and now they land a giant Arielle on top of me on the beach about a twenty-minute walk from my car.

We dragged the cases across the soft sand until we eventually managed to get the cases to the car. Then we went on to the St. Lawrence Hotel in Howth, a scenic, quiet peninsula only a fifteen-minute drive from my house. The hotel was close but far enough away to allow me to visit without anybody knowing.

It would be a good hideaway, a place to think through this impossible situation and plan my new double life. For the moment, I wasn't telling Isabel, Nobby or anybody else about my bizarre new situation.

The most beautiful, young, perfectly proportioned, 6'2" woman would be difficult to keep a secret, so as soon as I got the key to the room, we went straight to it and immediately, she began to unpack the most fabulous clothes.

'I've been doing my research, and the outfits I brought should be fashionable enough, but I will need your opinion,' she said, flashing a smile and winking at me.

'You did bring quite a lot,' I observed, seeing more and more stuff coming out of her small hand luggage which appeared to be bottomless.

So far, it looked as if she would need a double wardrobe to contain it all.

'I tuned into your media and watched a channel called Fashion TV. I watched all the shows, but my favourite of all was 'Lingerie'. I'm dying to go out wearing some.'

'You do realise lingerie is for wearing *under* your clothes?'

'Are you sure? I don't think you're right. All the girls in the show walked around in just lingerie and high-heeled shoes. I'll show you what I brought, starting with my lingerie, and then I will model my dresses, and you can tell me what you think.'

Arielle took some clothes out to the bathroom, soon arriving back in the sexiest black, satin, lacy lingerie. With her beautiful, long, golden hair and tanned, peachy skin, she now stood beside me, even taller, in stiletto heels.

Our eyes met at the same level.

We once had a loving relationship and I still had strong feelings for her, unable to help myself from taking the next step. I embraced her, then found I was without restraint.

We began to kiss, and soon, found ourselves making love on top of the king-sized double bed. Exhausted, we lay together, panting.

Arielle spoke first. 'That, Paddy, was wonderful. I have never experienced anything like that in my life. In Diaz, we have nothing that compares to sex. Procreation there happens in a laboratory. Wow! I felt the planet move … is that not an Earth saying?

'And did you enjoy it, Paddy? It was my first time. Am I the same as the other human females?' There were far too many questions at once.

'I don't know where you researched making love, but honestly, I'd say you're a natural! Arielle, you were wonderful.'

And then it struck me. *Oh my God, what have I done? I love my wife and my family, and need to be home for Sunday dinner.*

Arielle was eager, springing out of bed and returning to her luggage. 'I want to show you some more lingerie and maybe we can do the same thing again?'

Suddenly, she stopped rummaging, staring down at her tiny case.

'That was a big mistake.'

Still naked, I sat at the end of the bed, every sinew of me agreeing with her.

'It *was* a mistake. It should never have happened. I'm in love with Isabel and it's not right that I made love to you. At least it's good that we agree on it, Arielle.'

She turned to face me, scowling.

'That's not what I was talking about, I noticed as we were driving here that people wear a lot of casual clothes like jeans and tee-shirts, and I didn't bring any. That is what I say was a mistake. Other than that, Paddy, I am your devoted wife, and after careful deliberation and weighing all the consequences, I decided to get myself enlarged and changed to be a human woman so that we would fit nicely together.

'I decided to take a chance and travel here to be with you. I am still in love with you. I was lonely without you and hoped you would have the same feelings towards me.'

'Well, I do. I mean, I still feel the same way about you. The fact that you changed your whole body to come to help me … that means a lot to me … but so does my family, and I can't just cheat on them. They will always come first.'

'Please listen,' she implored me. 'I would like to say that regardless of everything that's happened to you, I respect you for staying grounded, always putting your wife and children first. But it is not as simple as that any longer. You didn't choose to be abducted. But you were. You didn't ask to be put on trial for the sins of mankind. But you were. You did ask to be freed and returned to Earth so that you could have the chance to right its wrongs. You *did* marry me, and now you have two wives.

'And that is a problem you will have to deal with, Paddy. So, you are going to have to come clean to Isabel and then tell your children and the whole world that you are a bigamist and your second wife is an alien being. What is difficult about that? It is simply honesty, that is all. And I'm sure you don't want this, but you have no choice.

'Caring for your own family just is not enough. You must care for all the creatures on earth and the environment too if you are to keep your family safe.

'Most people have accepted separation, divorce, the rights of children, gay rights, gay marriage. They can accept an alien wife. And the greater cause dictates that it is so, for now, it is time for rapid progress to legislate for the rights of animals and their habitats. We will work together to do what is needing to be done.

'I have come to Earth for one reason, because you are the only human I have ever met, and I love you dearly, so from this, I must assume that I love all humans. I have given up everything I have to be with you. There is no returning to Diaz for me.

'The body I have now cannot be reversed. I am prepared to give my life for humankind so that its collective sins can be undone.'

She waited quietly, rigid and staring. And far too tall for comfort. I had nothing to respond to this; what could I even say in response to these declarations?

Eventually, I could manage only, 'I … I just can't, Arielle. I'm sorry.'

She slumped as if about to deflate before me.

'Though I am your wife, I see that you reject me. Go now. Go home. But we will have to speak about it again because living with you is the sole solution for me.'

She pointed to the door and sobbed.

I got dressed and left.

***

Alone in the car park, I roared to the heavens. 'I really can't take any more of this!' How was I supposed to go home and tell Isabel that in addition to Nobby, an alien dog who was driving her insane, following her around the house staring at her, I now had an alien wife who was wanting to come home and sleep in our bed with us?

The first thing I needed to explain was how come I had shown up an hour late for Sunday dinner, an event that I had always insisted none of the family must not show up for. Checking my messages, indeed, the whole family was looking for me.

There seemed to be little point in telling lies at this stage.

***

When I pulled into the driveway, the door opened. Three teenagers and Kevin poured out. Isabel stayed at the threshold of the door, holding a twin in each arm.

The older kids were peering out at me.

'Where were you, Dad? What happened to you? Why didn't you answer your phone?' they interrogated. 'Mam thought you'd gone off with the aliens again!'

'Dinner's in the oven,' said Isabel icily. 'We decided to wait until you came home.'

'Let's eat! You must all be starving. I'll tell you afterwards.' I tried sounding upbeat.

The children served the meal.

Isabel sat at the opposite end of the table, staring at me with cold, severe eyes. Her knife and fork barely moved to touch her food.

I ate slowly, my stomach constricting, silently agonising over my words as I mulled over how to break the unpleasant and awkward news to them.

Isabel and I remained sitting at the table, looking at each other, while the children cleared it. I then asked them all to return to their dining seats.

I began, 'You know how I've been on TV, telling the world about having been abducted and where I got Nobby from, and my new stance on animal rights …'

'Yes,' Conan, our eldest, stated, nodding. 'Despite the ridicule we've all had to put up with, I'm sure that I can speak on behalf of all of us when I say we now accept everything you've said. Don't we?' he looked around. The kids pulled weird faces.

Whether it meant they really believed every word of it or were making fun of Dad, I wasn't sure, even now. Never mind; it had to be confronted, regardless.

'There's something I didn't get to tell you all about, because I thought it would be too far-fetched.'

'Go on,' Isabel prompted me in a most defeated tone that said, *here we go again.*

'Well, when I was in Diaz, I became an Irish singing and dancing star, performing in a musical which went viral across the entire planet. I started a sensation where everybody on the planet wanted to sing and dance to Irish music.

'I was helped by a Diazian female. Now, she's arrived on Earth with a belief that she can teach the people of Earth how to live on it sustainably. I was with her this afternoon, which is why I was late for dinner.'

'Ha, ha, ha! You're joking, right?' The children all laughed.

Isabel did not laugh, remaining stoney-faced and quiet.

'Where is the woman now?' she questioned.

'In a hotel in Howth.'

'These beings are knee-height, about the same as leprechauns, right?' she said, looking for confirmation.

'Well, they are when they're on Diaz, but Arielle—that's her name—went through some sort of a procedure. She's now 6'2".'

'Would you stop!'

The children could not stop laughing, clutching their sides and bellies.

Isabel was not amused. 'Right. Well, when can I meet her?' she asked with a pout.

'How about right now? She's alone in a hotel room, like I said. So, how about you kids look after the twins while Mam and I go there now?'

I had no way of letting Arielle know we were on our way, so she was surprised when she received a knock on her hotel door.

She opened it and saw us both standing there.

'This is my wife, Isabel. Can we come in?' I asked.

She opened the door, and we entered a standard-size hotel room with suitcases strewn around it. We all remained standing as the conversation began on the small floor space between the door and the end of the bed.

Isabel stared up at Arielle, 6'6" in her heels. Isabel was 5'7", wearing flats.

'I've become psychic recently,' voiced Isabel. 'I put it down to our new family pet from outer space. She follows me around all day, trying to stare into my eyes, and now I know why. Since Paddy claimed to have returned from his cosmic adventure, I knew there'd be a woman involved. Now, I finally get to meet his mistress.'

'Mistress? How dare you!' Arielle replied. 'I am his wife!'

Isabel screamed. 'Go back to where you came from!'

Arielle looked horrified—and weepy.

'We were married on Diaz,' she began, sobbing for the second time in hours. 'I thought since I loved Paddy, I would naturally love all humans, but since my arrival, I find that he only loves you. You don't want me either, and all I ever wanted to do was to be good to everybody. Oh Dear. This is a terrible mess.'

Arielle then slunk down onto the bed with her head in her hands and cried uncontrollably.

The pathetic sight of her brought me close to tears too.

Isabel, however, remained calm and sat on the bed, embracing and consoling her rival. 'Paddy, why don't you go for a walk?' she suggested. 'I'll phone you soon.'

Off I dutifully went, down to Howth Pier, leaving the women to it.

There, I sat on a bench, looking out to the sea. With dark, heavy clouds looming, and Ireland's Eye Island in the distance, I awaited the call to return.

It seemed like an interminable wait. Highly agitated by the suspense and with my imagination running wild, I could wait no longer.

I returned to the hotel and knocked on the door.

There was no answer.

My heart sank.

I jumped when my phone rang, sounding louder than usual.

'Paddy, where are you?' It was Isabel.

'I'm outside the door of the hotel room. I couldn't wait any longer.'

'We're in the hotel restaurant. Come and join us.'

When I arrived, they had both eaten starters and the main course and were laughing their way through a second bottle of wine.

'We both have the same size feet,' Isabel said, laughing. 'Her shoes fit me! We're both a size nine!'

Looking under the table, I noted that Isabel had borrowed Arielle's shoes and Arielle was in her bare feet.

'Did you see the clothes Arielle brought with her, Paddy? Now Arielle, I'm not saying that you don't look beautiful in them, but you'll need some sensible clothes too, so we're going shopping tomorrow.'

Arielle smiled, happy in the comfort that she now had a friend.

'Can somebody come with me to the toilet?' she asked. 'I'm not sure how it works.'

Isabel volunteered, and as I watched them crossing the restaurant, I noticed that every head in the room had turned to stare at Arielle's exceptional beauty and height.

We finished eating, and while walking Arielle back to her room, Isabel made arrangements to go to Dublin city with her the next day.

We said our goodbyes and returned to the car.

I put the key in the ignition, pausing before starting the car. 'I'm so sorry for putting you through all this, Isabel. It wasn't my fault! Things just happen to me!'

'No need to apologise. That's just you, Paddy. Besides, she's very nice and here to try and do good for all. I like her, and she's undoubtedly the most beautiful woman I've ever seen. Her accent's like no other I've ever heard too, melodious, with a very pleasant, friendly tone. I could listen to her all day. It's clear that she's fascinated by you, but it won't be long before a beauty like Arielle, who looks in her twenties, will tire of a balding fifty-something like yourself, and moves on to fresher pastures.'

I obviously had no response to this characteristically astute appraisal of the situation.

***

A few days later, all the family met Arielle. She told stories from the time we met, through to the time I departed her planet. They all loved her.

Chapter 20: Animal Lives

When Mrs Soft saw her only son, Norbert, battered and bruised after our night out, she vowed that, over her dead body would the two of us ever go out drinking together again. She said it was for our own good, making a rule that we should only meet during the day and bring Sinead, Isabel and children with us, instead of acting like drunken Yahoo's, she added.

We agreed, thinking that once the incident had become a distant memory, we could go back to our old ways. We arranged for our families to go shopping in Dublin, and then to meet up in our auld favourite pub, Tommy Byrne's, for a meal.

The adults sat at one table and the children at another. The twins, now one year old, had been left with their grandparents.

'This is where the night started,' Sinead reminded Isabel, giggling. '*The boys are back in town; the boys are back in town …*'

She started to sing the old Thin Lizzy classic.

We laughed.

Everyone else laughed too but for Mrs Soft, who didn't find it one bit amusing.

She sat rigidly and reminded us that we were nearly sixty years old and ought to be ashamed of ourselves. 'Honestly, the two of you! If you were respectable men, you would have been at home in your slippers with your families, but, oh no! Paddy and Nobby are out brawling in a nightclub. So, tell me something new for a change.'

I hid my face behind the menu, and then I read: *Chicken wings, baby back pork ribs!* Why had we arranged to eat here again?

Gavin, the owner, came over to take our orders. 'Well, well. I *am* honoured to serve the famous Paddy O'Reilly,' he said with a warm smile.

'Am I?' I asked. 'Famous for what?'

'For being in outer space.'

'What else?' I asked.

'Animal rights,' he replied.

'Well, if that is so, what are you doing offering me tortured animals for lunch?' I stood, my finger pointing at him like a gun.

'You don't have to eat them if you don't want to.'

'And you don't have to serve them, do you?'

Mrs Soft got to her feet. 'Paddy O'Reilly, sit down immediately! Would you believe it? It's not even safe to go for Sunday lunch with you without courting disaster. There's plenty of other food on the menu. Look, nachos, vegetarian curry, salad bar. Eat those. You're making a show of us all!'

A chorus of *sit down!* came from both tables, so I did, but I'd made my point, and no chicken or pork dishes were ordered.

When we finished eating, I ushered Nobby up to a bar stool and leaned in, speaking low into his ear.

'You'll never guess.' His brows went up. 'Arielle's here, from outer space.'

'No, come on!' he said. 'You've become delusional. Next, you'll be telling me you met Goldilocks and the three bears.'

'I'm telling you, boy! She's already met the family and she's coming here. She'll be here any minute, actually. Brace yourself, Nobby … She's the most beautiful woman you've ever seen. Oh, and she's 6'2" in flats but likes to wear heels.'

'Would you feck off! What sort of an eejit do you think I am?'

The door opened and all 6'6" of Arielle walked into the bar.

Nobby's jaw dropped, and he stood with his mouth open as she made her way over.

'Hi, Arielle,' I said. 'Good to see you.' I kissed her on the cheek. 'I'd like to introduce you to my best friend, Nobby.'

They shook hands.

Isabel came over and introduced Arielle to the remainder of Nobby's family.

Arielle explained where she was from and why she had come to Earth.

I suggested all meeting at our house for dinner the following Sunday and that's what we did.

***

There were twelve people to dinner: Nobby and Sinead and their three teenagers; Isabel and our three teenagers; and Kevin, who was to be a teenager next birthday. Isabel had decided that twelve was too large a crowd for inside the house, so we decided to eat outside on our large deck which was the width of our semi-detached.

We brought out the rectangular dining table, which was the same dimensions as our outdoor table, placing them end to end.

Arielle and I sat halfway along the row of six chairs on one side.

Nobby's son, Joe, the eldest of the teenagers, looked at me from across the table, and asked, 'So what are we supposed to eat, then?'

Me and my friends like pizza, steaks, chicken wings and fish and chips.

I could tell he was annoyed by the idea of going without meat.

'Joe, we are not suggesting going without meat, just to eat less meat and only meat that has been reared out in the fields the way nature intended. Eat free range chicken and the slices of salami on your pizza from pigs that have been raised outdoors. Beef for your burgers is all raised from outdoor raised cattle and fish from the sea is free range too. You learned to accept covid lockdowns, eating less meat will be easy'.

'All right, so,' he said, sounding less than enthusiastic.

A discussion on how to get our point across to the public continued throughout the afternoon and into the evening until the sun went down.

More publicity was needed. What better way of achieving that than to introduce Arielle, the intergalactic beauty, to the whole world?

And where better to start in Ireland than the *Late, Late Show*?

***

I contacted the host, Mick O'Toole, telling him about the latest twist in the story.

We were immediately invited on the show.

I sat alone on the couch while Mick briefly recapped my story in advance of the main event. 'And now, I would like to introduce almost certainly the most special guest we have ever had on the show … Arielle the leprechaun fairy girl who underwent drastic surgery to change her into a giant …!'

The audience laughed.

Arielle entered the stage, 6'6", wearing her sexy stilettos and one of her most revealing Fashion TV dresses. She certainly was not looking like a leprechaun.

The audience, instantly entranced, watched in awed silence as Arielle took to the stage with sublime elegance and sensuality.

She then seated herself beside me on the couch.

Mick, caught like a rabbit in headlights, took a few moments to compose himself.

The camera zoomed in on Arielle's face to capture her mysterious royal blue eyes, immediately suggesting that she wasn't quite the same as anybody from this planet.

Mick began, obviously mesmerised by her beauty, and asked the first of his stupid prepared questions: 'Are all the girls from your planet as hot as you are? If so, could you organise an invasion?'

The audience laughed.

'We are all different,' she replied, straight-faced.

'Why are you here?' he asked.

'I met Paddy after he was abducted and fell in love with him. I believed that all humans would be like him, so I came here to save them all.'

'SAVE US! Save us from what?'

'Some extra-terrestrials believe that humans are a very low form of life and should be exterminated, or at the very least, the males should be castrated so that in time, the race would die out.

'Their understanding of the nature of humans is based upon the premise that if your intellect and cunning were to evolve to such an extent that you became capable of inter-galactic travel, fear and havoc would be wrought throughout the galaxies.

'In short, they are afraid of the destructive power of humanity. The immense potential to ruin, something you have already shown. You have already turned the Earth's atmosphere into a rubbish tip with satellite debris circling the planet. What sort of damage would the human race be capable of if it were let loose into the universe?'

'And here we are, worried about global warming!' Mick riposted, inanely, with his hands on his head.

'Global warming. That's easy for our advanced technology to fix,' she replied. 'We have the technology to allow those greenhouse gases to escape through Earth's atmosphere into space. But even if global warming is solved, what other problems will lead to the demise of humans? It's what humans need to become which is the real issue. Treat each other as you would like to be treated yourself. Love your neighbour. That must include all the plants and all animals. If it lives, you must respect it.'

Arielle's charismatic poise charmed the audience.

***

After the show had finished, I drove Arielle back to her hotel room.

She asked me to stay, but I told her I had to get home to my family and left her watching TV, something she spent a lot of time doing.

Animal documentaries, sports, music, the arts. Her favourite show, however, was 'Love Island'. We found out later that she had applied to be a contestant.

The children were watching Episode 5 of 'Love Island 2025' when we heard excitement emanating from the lounge.

'Dad, Mam, come quickly! It's Arielle! She's on television!'

All the contestants had partnered up, and it seemed that most were happy with their choices. They were, that is, until Arielle was introduced to the house as a 'bombshell'. This meant that, according to the rules of the show, participants could opt to exchange their current chosen partner for another.

Each man stepped forward to swap out their former selections for Arielle.

She made her choice too but continued to change partners until six episodes before the final, when she found her soul mate, a sensitive, man who shared her views on life. Meanwhile, she had captivated 'Love

Island' and its devoted viewers. The final vote was just a contest of who came second, third and fourth.

Everybody knew that Arielle, accompanied by her gentle beau, Ronnie, would win.

***

Thanks to Arielle, AL—Animal Lives —became a worldwide social movement setting about opening people's eyes to the barbarity of intensive factory farming, showing the way caged animals were treated.

We insisted that animals were intelligent, had emotions and deserved a natural life.

Arielle's new-found fame allowed her to speak on the subject all over the world, the public listening to our arguments. The popularity of AL grew.

We were then approached by the major sports brands of the world, who showed an interest in being associated with AL.

Logos were designed in support of the movement. The great rock and sports stars of the world were the first to wear them, publicly promoting the cause.

People no longer felt awkward about giving their opinion on animal rights. In fact, the wearing of the logos became fashionable.

Fashion, usually limited to frivolous vanity, was now being seen in the honourable light of promoting the cause of justice for animals.

By the year 2028, the focus of education had changed to how to live life well and what a person's responsibility should be as a citizen of Earth. Individual academic achievement followed this. Animal welfare and care for the environment became core subjects to be studied at elementary education.

People ate less meat. Farmers, worldwide, were paid twice as much to produce half the amount of ethically raised stocks. It all made such sense. Smaller herds led to fewer methane emissions, so this major cause of greenhouse gas was now in decline.

Giving rights to animals started an age of enlightenment in which it was agreed, worldwide, to give animals back their habitats to which man had no right anyway.

All nations were encouraged by a social welfare system to have small families.

Nature reserves and wilderness directives targeted the halting and reversing of the loss of biodiversity. In the following years, there was a steady increase in the populations of birds, insects, bees, fish and all animals, as well as forest growth.

Since intensive farming became banned, there was no cross-contamination of disease between species and because of this, no new pandemics occurred.

A small, but steady decrease in the human population resulted, leaving enough renewable energy to power the smaller world.

The use of fossil fuels ended, and with it, the threat of global warming.

Nations united. Race, colour and creed were no longer causes of division, as all people believed they were as one, a single species. The Human. *Homo Sapiens.* Us.

A species that could expect more visits from extra-terrestrials.

Chapter 21: Lake Naivasha 2040

The air was still and balmy.

I blew smoke rings from my small cigar and watched them slowly dissipate, uninterrupted by any breeze.

Sitting alone on a rocking chair, I drifted into the seventh degree of concentration while listening to the soft, soothing sounds of chirping crickets.

I stared at my right big toe, broken twice, and deformed. An ulcerated vein, caused by the stamping of a rugby boot from the distant past, throbbed on my left shin.

Both knees ached. I needed new ones.

My hips needed replacing, and my back was killing me.

Darkness had fallen, the low calls of the African night reverberating back and forth. The low whooping of a hyena turned to a ghostly wail.

That's enough, isn't it? I've done everything I ever wanted to do and seen everything I ever wanted to see. Nobody depends on me now. In fact, old and decrepit, I'm increasingly becoming a burden on others.

I made my way to the car park and started the jeep, driving along a dirt trail to the dimly lit wooden jetty where the day's safari had begun.

Time to feed the animals. It's their turn to eat now.

The lights of the jeep beamed brightly off the end of the jetty out into the lake as I took off my shoes, socks, trousers and shirt.

I felt I was being watched as I began to slowly lower myself down a ladder into the cold lake water. My teeth chattered as I doggie-paddled out into the depths until I could swim no further.

That's it. The point of no return.

I panicked, suddenly afraid of what I was about to do and tried to swim back. I attempted the front crawl, but in my feeble state, was not able to keep it up for long. I was soon exhausted and choking. There was no getting back to shore now. This was indeed the end. I let myself be taken by the lake and eventually floated face down in it.

I had always heard that your entire life flashed in front of you the second before you would die. For me, it began with the roars of the schoolboys, cheering me on during the school day fights. Then there was the bark and green leaves of the silver birch tree in the back garden. My grandmother's hands and her skin seemed to be timeless.

I guessed people would never understand and would be upset and disappointed when they found out what I had done but all I was doing was moving to another plain of existence then familiar to me.

From the heavens above, Isabel's voice called to me.

Calmly, I looked down at my discarded body as my spirit floated upwards.

Beside me was my angel, Isabel, carrying me up with her right arm around my back and my left over hers.

As we peacefully ascended, we turned to look at each other. She looked as she had on the day I'd first met her on Fitzwilliam Square, dressed in winter clothes with the same beany hat and scarf covering her nose and mouth showing just her beautiful brown eyes.

My last view of Earth was the lake and the writhing mass of hungry, rolling crocodiles, tearing my limbs from my empty body. Crocodiles gotta eat meat too.

Please review my book ...

Dear Reader,

I hope you enjoyed my book. If so, I hope you don't mind if I ask you to please write a review on Amazon or on any platform on which you discovered it. Many readers do not realise that the success of an author is greatly enhanced by receiving reviews, no matter the content!

Thank you so much,

Bobby Brazil, (Dublin, 17.03.24).

Printed in Great Britain
by Amazon